THE PRINCE'S DANGEROUS WISH

A CLEAN FANTASY FAIRY TALE RETELLING OF THE PINK

THE NEVERTOLD FAIRY TALE NOVELLAS
BOOK TWO

BRITTANY FICHTER

To Hope,

We always said it would take a special woman to keep up with my brother, and I'm so grateful that he found that woman in you. You're lovely, strong, and steady, and if this world had a lot more like you, it would be a far better place.

CONTENTS

TO THE HONORABLE KING EVERARD AND QUEEN ISABELLE,

This second tale is a bit different from the first, in that our hero in peril is a prince, rather than a princess. Peter says this story was born long ago when he saw just such an event happen to the son of a powerful duke. He also claims that at one time, the fae weren't nearly so selfish as most are now, and a choice group of them were even gifted incredible powers by the Maker with the express purposes of helping the humble of the world.

Tiger Lily was particular fond of this story. She liked hearing about the powerful, regal faeries who were generous and misjudged by men. I'm under the impression that she saw herself as such a benefactor to Peter, the Lost Boys, and all the other fae. Thankfully, the story I'm about to tell has a different ending than the one she met with. But I shouldn't get ahead of myself. You can draw your own conclusions for yourselves.

Yours respectfully,
Wendy Darling Pan

Once upon a time in a faraway land...

CHAPTER
ONE

Nadine stared morosely out the window at the crowd mingling in the palace gardens below. They all looked so confident. So happy. So perfect. The ladies giggled and peeked coyly from behind their fans, and the men stood tall, laughing and boasting together. They were so loud she could hear them through the glass.

"Your Highness!"

Nadine turned to see Alicia, her first lady, bustling in and looking quite frazzled. "We've been looking all over for you!"

Nadine looked back down at the party. "I know," she said in a soft voice.

Alicia, usually the picture of grace and calm sophistication, glanced nervously down at the party too. "I... I'm afraid, Your Highness, that the king is very anxious to see you."

Nadine heaved a deep sigh and nodded before she slowly stood. "Very well. Thank you for fetching me." She walked to the door then paused a moment to go through her mother's instructions in her head. Though Nadine had lived in the palace for nine months now, her mother's sharp commands were as clear in her head as they had been when she was thirteen.

Chin up.

Shoulders back.

Stomach taut.

Mouth relaxed.

Eyes distant.

"Oh!" Alicia exclaimed, hurrying toward her again. "Let me fix your hair!"

Nadine waited patiently until her first lady was finished, then she made her way through the door.

Though the stately gait and expression were as familiar to her as her own skin, Nadine always felt as though she were hiding behind an invisibility charm as she put on the persona of queen.

But that wasn't necessarily a bad thing. If she could wear the persona as well as her mother believed she should, it meant the true Nadine was hidden safely beneath. The courtiers could judge and gossip all they wanted. They were criticizing a woman who didn't exist. As long as Nadine made sure not to crack, not to reveal any weakness beneath, she could stay that way.

Safe and unknown.

If only her husband were so easy to fool, she thought as

she made her way down the castle's main front stairs.

King Albert was not a bad-looking man. And upon first introduction, he was all that was pleasing. Charming, tasteful compliments. Witty jokes and clever insights. He could sum a man up five minutes after meeting him.

But that had been the trouble. He'd sized her up well the day they'd met. He'd quickly sorted out Nadine's fears and anxieties. He'd even commented on how life as queen would be difficult for someone like her, someone who struggled to read those around her, who tired easily when there were too many people around her.

"You're an odd little beauty, aren't you?" he'd chuckled as they'd first walked through the very garden Nadine was entering now.

And yet, he'd made one mistake.

He had believed her capable of change.

But Nadine had not changed. Not when the entire palace had descended upon her to prepare her for the wedding. Not when her mother had threatened her severely if she dared hint to the king that she wanted to call the wedding off. Not even when the king had–to his credit–kindly hired a master of manners to help her conquer her struggles with crowds and attention.

Nadine was the same shy, timid girl she had been before her mother forced her to meet the king. But as long as she could keep that girl tucked away, secretly hidden beneath the veneer of the perfect queen, she would be safe.

As long as the king let her.

"There you are, my beauty!" Albert boomed as Nadine

entered the garden. He quickly made his way to her side and bowed low, kissing her hand. Nadine fell into a curtsey that perfectly matched her husband's chivalry. She smiled sweetly at him and batted her eyes.

"My apologies, my lord," she said. "My hair didn't wish to present itself today." This wasn't a lie. Nadine had left it that way on purpose until Alicia had so kindly intervened.

A woman nearly as tall as Nadine's husband stood behind him. Her hair, black with several streaks of silver, was perfectly curled and pinned, a fact she seemed aware of as she peered unsmiling down her aquiline nose at her daughter-in-law.

The king, seeming unaware of his mother's obvious disapproval, boomed another laugh. "If we can't wait for the queen on her own birthday, who can we wait on? Come this way, my love. Your people desire to celebrate with you."

"Remember," the queen mother said in a low voice, "the Stules wish to discuss an acquisition before they go."

"Did they get the legal permits from King Stephan?" the king murmured back.

His mother's eyes narrowed. "If he doesn't know the land is his, does it even matter?"

Albert nodded thoughtfully then returned his attention to his wife and guests.

Nadine had no desire to celebrate with their guests or play the pretty maiden to her mother-in-law's obsession with land acquisitions. But she had little choice. So she continued to smile as if she'd heard nothing.

Of course, it wasn't that she was ungrateful for her

guests' lavish gifts, or the opulent palace decorations, or even the towering cake her husband had ordered the kitchens to prepare for her. Nor was she ignorant of the fact that Albert really did seem to be trying to make her happy. He had done everything he could think of to make this party enjoyable. And it probably would have been...

If Nadine were like him.

But she wasn't. She was, however, a fantastic pretender. So she feigned her best simpering smile as her husband led her enthusiastically through the sea of people clamoring for her attention, eager to assure their new queen that she could find court allies in them. And Nadine smiled and nodded and said all the right things. Her mother had spent so much time drilling the correct answers into her that she hardly had to think about them anymore. They just came out, even when Nadine was perfectly aware that the simpering ladies before her had been gossiping behind her back just moments earlier when they didn't think she was listening.

"My dear," Albert said cheerfully, drawing her from her momentary reverie. He gestured toward a very tall, very thin man. "This is our new menagerie keeper. I mentioned that you like studying the animals there, and he helped me create a gift I think you'll particularly enjoy."

Nadine shifted her perfect persona slightly so she could peek at the tall man's outstretched hands with true interest. And when he opened his cupped hands, she gasped in delight.

Enclosed in a clear circle of glass no larger than her thumb was a tiny blue butterfly. When the thin man shifted his hands from side-to-side, the blue shimmered slightly into purple and then back again. The flat circle of glass was attached to a gold chain, and Nadine genuinely beamed as the king took it from the thin man's hands, and after removing the necklace she was wearing, fastened the chain around her neck.

"It's lovely," she breathed, lifting the pendant to see it more closely. "How ever did you get it in its Pixiant stage?"

The thin man's brows went up. "The queen knows her magical creatures well."

"Queen Nadine," a thin, high voice said, "excels in knowledge of animals and magical creatures." The woman who embodied the voice joined their little circle. Her smile was wide, but Nadine had to stop herself from physically recoiling as the woman came to stand at her side. "I believe it's one of her greatest passions."

"Good afternoon, Lady Chrysanthemum," Nadine said, clinging a little tighter to her husband's arm.

"Your Highness," Lady Chrysanthemum cooed with a curtsey. Though they hadn't been rivals for nearly a year–the time when the king had chosen his queen–Nadine doubted Lady Chrysanthemum would let her forget anytime soon that she had been one of Nadine's closest competitors.

If she was honest, Nadine was still just as perplexed as Lady Chrysanthemum seemed to be as to why Albert had chosen her.

The thin man, seemingly unaware of the snideness in Lady Chrysanthemum's tone, looked back at Nadine again.

"In that case, please send word anytime Her Majesty wishes to stroll through the menagerie. I'll make sure my most knowledgeable workers are there to discuss any animal you would seek."

Despite the rude courtier, Nadine felt herself smiling again. "That would be most enjoyable." She turned to her husband. "We could spend quite a happy evening there together." And though she kept her tone appropriately uninterested, Nadine knew as soon as his eyes flicked away from hers that she had shared too much.

Albert gave her a polite smile and a slight bow. "Whatever pleases my lady." He gestured to the other side of the garden. "Now, I should greatly like to introduce you to..."

But Nadine didn't hear him. She knew he had no intention of going to the menagerie. And though his gift had been exactly the kind to touch her heart, she knew she had pushed too far. The young queen's odd fixation with animals, magical and non-magical alike, had been one of the first topics of gossip to roar through the court like wildfire. And now that Albert had retreated to the courteous, proper husband a king was supposed to be...

Nadine had no choice but to retreat, too.

Unfortunately, the party didn't improve as it aged. Far from it, Nadine felt her mask begin to slip little by little as she continued to mingle and greet her subjects. She felt her perfect posture slump slightly as her fatigued shoulders and back protested. The heavy skirts she wore made her steps slower and more awkward, and she could tell that the longer she exerted her false self, the more frustrated her husband became.

Eventually, she knew she could go on no more. Her stomach was unbelievably queasy, and she felt like she was running out of air. How was it hot and cold at the same time? Was she having a heart spasm?

"My dear," she said to her husband, dredging up a smile once more, "I'm feeling a bit fatigued. Would you mind if I went to refresh myself for a few minutes? I think my hair needs Lady Alicia's help once more in this heat."

For the first time in hours, Albert's face lit up with approval. "Of course, my dear. Make yourself as ready as you please. I'll be waiting for you out here."

Nadine smiled and bid her current visitors farewell. Then, in a move perfected by years of evading her mother at similar events, she managed to lose not just Alicia, but all of her ladies-in-waiting. Hidden in the shadows now cast by the evening light, she ran to the only place where she could breathe freely.

A corner of the menagerie wasn't far from the garden where the party was being held. It was quiet, as most of the animals inside were sleeping. And though the main doors were locked, Nadine knew of a side gate the animal keepers used to get in and out. She stealthily slipped through the gate, which had been left slightly ajar, and made her way to her favorite roofless enclosure in the corner. Aware of her delicate fabric and silk shoes, Nadine sank onto a small rise in the grass and rested her back against the wall.

Most of the gnomes were asleep piled against one

another in the opposite corner of the enclosure. Their clothes, which were sewn by several of the women in the city, gave their collective group the impression of a small hill of blue and green. And though they much resembled humans–stout, bearded humans that came up to Nadine's knee–they couldn't have spoken to Nadine even if they were awake. This, of course, was one of the reasons Nadine had chosen this particular enclosure.

One of the gnomes, which had been sleeping at the edge of the pile, startled slightly at the sound of Nadine's soft sigh. When his eyes met hers, he beamed. Then he stood and waddled over to her, and she smiled and held open her arms. He toddled right over and half-sat, half-fell into her lap, where he immediately curled up and fell asleep again, his little beard rising and falling with his snores. Nadine smiled and shifted him into a more comfortable position. Holding a gnome was much like snuggling a toddler that had the personality of an enthusiastic cat.

"You act as though queens steal into your room every day to rest," Nadine laughed softly. She rubbed the little gnome's neck as she took deep, calming breaths.

She ought to go back to the party soon. And probably ought to stop by her room in truth if she was to fool her guests. Sitting in a menagerie stall certainly wasn't doing any favors for her hair. But every time she decided she should return, she convinced herself to stay just half a minute longer. Half a minute wasn't really so much. Was it?

Nadine woke up to the bang of wood on wood. She blinked rapidly to clear her vision as a young boy gaped at her from the door of the enclosure. They stared at one another until Nadine was hit by a sickening realization.

The party.

She had forgotten to return to her own party.

The boy seemed to remember himself at about the same time because he leaned back and shouted over his shoulder,

"I found her! The queen's in with the gnomes!"

Nadine opened her mouth to beg him not to say such a thing, but she was too late. She heard a crowd rush into the menagerie. And to her horror, not only did she find herself peeking up at guards who stood on the other side of the fence, but party guests as well. The women looked like they might burst with glee, and the men seemed utterly confused.

Worst of all, however, was the face of her husband. Anger, embarrassment, and frustration warred in his eyes. She could tell it was with great difficulty that he kept his voice calm and cheerful as he turned to address his guests.

"It looks like Her Highness wasn't able to stay away from her birthday present."

Nadine stared at him. What was he talking about?

"I was going to announce it later," Albert continued, chuckling as if it was all an endearing situation, "but I brought several new gnomes into the menagerie recently.

May all you husbands be so fortunate as to gift your wives with presents they can't ignore."

The men laughed, and the women tittered appropriately, but Nadine knew this wouldn't be forgotten any time soon by either her husband or the court. Forcing a rueful smile, she allowed her husband to help her stand. They followed their guests out of the menagerie, but as before they crossed the threshold, he bent low and put his mouth to her ear. When he spoke, his voice was not kind.

"We need to talk."

CHAPTER
TWO

As soon as Nadine's bedchamber door was shut and locked, and the king had gone through every room in her chambers to make sure they were alone, he turned to face her. Nadine tried to steel herself for what was coming. She'd had countless such confrontations with her mother before getting married, and had hoped that her days of being lectured were over now that she was out of her parents' house.

But, apparently, she had been wrong.

She half-expected him to start shouting and braced herself for such. But instead of shouting, he simply closed his eyes and pinched the bridge of his nose.

The sound of a cricket somewhere in the corner grew louder and louder as Nadine waited, and she could hear the slightly raucous laughter rising from the party below. But after half a minute, Nadine decided that the silence was worse than any yelling would have been.

"I understand," he finally said, opening his eyes and facing her, "that large parties are distasteful to you. But for this one night, I thought... I thought you would be able to do your duty as queen."

"I–"

"Just. *One*. Night," he said, his gray eyes growing colder.

Nadine flinched. "I didn't ask for a party," she said. The words came out sounding more petulant than she meant them to.

"We don't ask for many things!" Albert exploded. "But they come with a crown. Obligations come with a crown! Or didn't your mother tell you that?"

"She did."

"Then why are you so surprised when duty is required of you?"

"I wasn't surprised!" she pulled an offending pin out of her hair and tossed it on her vanity. "I did the best that I could. I laughed. I talked. I mingled. All I wanted was a few minutes' peace before I had to go back." She huffed. "I never meant to fall asleep."

"I certainly *hope* you didn't." He rubbed his chin. Then he shook his head and sighed. "As I told you when we married, I understand your...your dislike for large parties and gatherings. But our personal dislikes cannot keep us from doing what we must." He walked over to the window. "Tonight, for example, I had nearly confirmed the purchase of land on our northern border. It would have expanded our territory to encompass the river. And Sir Romin had nearly agreed to contribute a good sum of money to our expansive enterprises on the southwest coast." He turned back to her. "But then his wife asked where you were, and panic nearly broke loose when no one could find you."

In spite of herself, shame heated Nadine's cheeks. "As I said, I didn't mean to fall asleep. I only meant to take a few minutes' respite before returning."

Her husband's eyes opened wide. "You were tired?" He glanced at her midsection. "Could you be–"

"No," she retorted crossly. "I am not. And I know that for a fact."

He said nothing, but his shoulders slumped slightly.

"And to your earlier point, my discomfort with large gatherings isn't a...*dislike* exactly."

"No?" he asked.

"No." She frowned, trying to find the words she could never quite say to her mother. If only she could show them, rather than tell them, what it felt like when so many eyes were on her. When she had person after person acting and reacting before her, and she was supposed to interpret their intentions through expressions and coy words. She had to read faces and interpret body movements, all faster than she could come up with words to respond. It was why she had memorized so many shallow phrases as a girl, which had led to many a possible suitor simply thinking her daft.

"You are a quick judge of character," she said slowly. "You understand not only what people say but what they intend, even if they don't say it. I'm not like that, though." She looked up to him, hoping beyond hope that maybe...just maybe he would understand what her mother never had. "I have a hard time knowing what people mean. So often they say one thing but mean another. And while I'm trying to puzzle out what the person in front of me is trying to really say, three more are thrust upon me, and I'm expected to understand and respond to them all at the same time."

She shrugged. "I know you disapprove of my attachment to animals. I know it's not a queenly pastime to spend so much time with them. But animals...Animals aren't like people. They don't say one thing and do another." She gathered the courage to look her husband in the eyes once more. "Sometimes I need that."

Her husband, who had been frowning thoughtfully at her, stared a moment longer before pulling in a deep breath through his nose, then letting it back out again. When he spoke, his voice was soft. But even she could see the disappointment written clearly on his face.

"The crown may have needs. But the crown *must* do as the people need. Whether we feel ourselves capable of it or not."

"Well, then maybe the crown should have chosen a woman who actually wanted to be queen!" Nadine snapped.

As soon as the words were out of her mouth, she wished with all her heart that she could take them back. But she couldn't. So instead of trying to clean up the mess she'd made, she bolted past him and threw herself, weeping, onto the reclining sofa in her parlor.

Albert said nothing as he left her chambers, nor did he send any other word after. And the first shame of the evening's earlier escapade was quickly forgotten as Nadine relived her hurtful words again and again in her head.

It was true that her husband demanded much of her. Her last year had seen her nearly constantly exhausted. But he had always been far more gentle with her than her mother ever was. And while Nadine had never desired to be queen, it was also true that she did care for the man she had married. For a marriage of convenience, she had found herself relatively happy, surrounded by all the comforts and luxuries of the world and spoiled by her husband, even if his gifts were somewhat misguided. At least, unlike a number of her friends' husbands, he was faithful.

And now she had ruined it all.

A soft whirring and gentle breeze made Nadine look up from the cushion in which she'd buried her face. She nearly fell off the sofa when she realized that she was no longer alone.

"Good evening, dear," the woman said with a smile.

Nadine tried to respond, but her mouth couldn't seem to catch up with her mind. The woman standing before her was several inches taller than she was and as beautiful as the night was dark. Her skin seemed to give off its own soft glow, and her blue wings shimmered with the barest hint of pastel colors that changed as she moved them. Her hair was pulled up into an elaborate twist, and there were gems scattered throughout it. In her hand was a wand that shimmered brighter than all the rest. It might have been made of one large sapphire for all Nadine knew.

"You're—" Nadine managed to gasp, but the woman smiled again and stepped closer.

"I'm Healanie," the woman said, taking a step closer. "And I know that you are Nadine, new queen of Tuilidad, daughter of Lord Gaston and Lady Victoria." She paused, her brows furrowing slightly. "And I've been watching King Albert's line long enough that tonight convinced me that it's time to act."

Nadine blinked up at her. "Tonight—"

"Was only the most recent in a line of incidents of which I didn't approve...most of which you're absolutely ignorant." She pursed her slightly shimmering pink lips. "But I expect little less, considering how awful his parents were and his grandparents before them. Compared to them, he's a saint."

Nadine hastily wiped her wet cheeks on her sleeves while scrambling to sit up. "I didn't mean to...I spoke in haste, my lady faerie. My husband isn't a bad man."

"You did speak in haste, it's true. And you did hurt him, which I am glad you take credit for. Your words were unkind. And you are right, he is not a bad man as the term is generally used." She leaned slightly forward. "But what if I told you he could become even better?"

"What?" Nadine stared at her blankly. Tuilidad was generally friendly to faeries, and her husband had even spoken with the faerie queen several times. But Nadine knew the danger of making deals with faeries. And while her husband may not understand her, Nadine had no desire to foist a mischievous faerie upon him. The consequences could be dire.

"Of course," Healanie leaned back and studied Nadine. "It will be difficult. No true change can be had without difficulty. Otherwise, the change would have already been made. Yes, I think I will."

She broke into a triumphant smile once more. "I also happen to know that while your husband is hurt, I have the perfect gift with which to cheer him." Her lavender eyes sparkled. Then she leaned back and lifted her chin triumphantly. "And not long after you receive this gift, you will know that none like it has ever been given by a faerie before."

Before Nadine could respond, the faerie lifted her wand and waved it over Nadine's head several times. Then she beamed and nodded once.

"What kind of gift?" Nadine finally managed to ask.

"There's no need to look so terrified, love," the faerie laughed. "Oh, but before I go, I need to warn you of one thing." Her smile disappeared. "Make sure to take care with the gift. If you do not steward it well, it could be the death of you."

And with that, she was gone.

NADINE WAITED up the rest of the night (or what was left of it) to receive her gift. But nothing came. Nor did it come the next day. Or the next. Or the next.

Unfortunately, as she expected and—to her own admission—somewhat deserved, the king was cold with her in the weeks that followed. He was always polite. But the warmth was missing from his eyes. His smile was never as genuine as it had once been when she greeted him.

Four months later, Nadine had all but given up on the faerie's promised gift when she woke up one morning and, as usual, allowed her ladies-in-waiting to dress her. During this ritual, one of the younger ladies cried out in surprise,

"Your Majesty! Your dress! It won't fit!"

Nadine, whose mind had been elsewhere, turned to look at the mirror and was both shocked and overjoyed to see that her belly seemed to have grown quite round overnight. One of her other ladies-in-waiting squealed, and Alicia had to grow quite severe before the other young women could be brought to order.

Her ladies caused such a stir that Nadine was sure word would spread like wildfire within the hour. So once more appropriate clothes had been acquired, Nadine sent word to request her husband's presence before he could hear the news from anyone else. Her ladies had been sworn to secrecy, but she didn't trust the gossip chain to slow one bit.

The king was announced an hour later. Thankfully, Alicia had shooed the other ladies into another room to do some unnecessary cleaning. More likely to keep them from gossiping than anything else, Nadine guessed with profound gratefulness.

"You need me, my queen?" he asked in his polite, distant tone as the door closed behind him. Nadine, who was lying on her parlor couch, tried to keep her words from sounding breathless.

"I did, my love."

As he turned to her, the king's brows rose high at the term of endearment, but as soon as he faced her completely, he stopped and stared.

"Nadine," he whispered, his eyes locked on her. It was the first time he'd used her given name since her birthday. "Are you..." He stopped and licked his lips. "Do we have an heir?"

Nadine nodded at him happily, not even needing to pretend happiness this time.

After that, it was as if they had never squabbled at all. As if Nadine had never said such hurtful words and the king had never given her those awful looks of disappointment. Her husband was all kindness, all gentleness as he kissed her hands and face again and again, exclaiming what a good mother she would be and how much joy this announcement would bring to the kingdom.

Basking in the happiness of feeling close to her husband once more, and soon after, the sensation of her baby's kicks, Nadine forgot the warning of the faerie Haelanie. But she was reminded of it all too soon after her son was born.

CHAPTER

THREE

N adine had a decent idea of what her son's gift was from an early age. She wondered years later why the magic changed, requiring him to use particular words once he was verbal, but allowing him more variance when he was small. It mattered little, though, for once he was able to speak, her fears were confirmed. The faerie hadn't been exaggerating the danger her gift brought with it, and not much time passed before Nadine would have done nearly anything to give the gift back.

Rolf had the sweetest disposition Nadine had ever seen in a baby, which was probably why the palace didn't burn down during his first two years of life. He cried as often as any infant, but his tantrums were few and far between, much to his mother's great relief. Unfortunately, just before his first birthday, Nadine was forced to admit that what she feared most was really true.

The boy had been playing quietly on the rug beside his

mother as she penned a letter to a cousin, excusing their lack of attendance at the cousin's wedding by citing her son's fragile health, the general excuse that allowed her to keep him away from the court and other large gatherings.

"No one who saw you for more than five minutes would believe it." Nadine looked over at him with a wry smile. "You are the strongest, healthiest little boy I've ever seen."

Rolf looked up at her and gurgled at her through a big, drooly grin.

"And I do hate to lie," she murmured, looking back at the letter. "But I don't know how to explain the truth." She peeked back at her son again. "You truly leave me without words."

To explain that her son was faerie gifted would be nothing less than to invite trouble, especially as faeries had so rarely blessed the children of her husband's line.

"Mama," he said, holding his chubby little hands out to her.

"Just a moment, darling," she said distantly, reading over her letter again.

"*Mama!*" he said again. But this time, it was not a request. It was very similar to the tone his father used when issuing orders in the throne room. Nadine let out a little scream as her chair tipped her sideways, dumping her onto the floor beside the baby and spilling the bottle of ink in her lap. She was still staring open-mouthed at the mess when Alicia rushed in.

"Is everything–Your Highness! Are you well?" She hurried to help Nadine to her feet.

"Um, yes. I mean, please get me some water," Nadine said, trying to sound more coherent than she felt. "I...I think I feel a little faint."

Alicia called one of the younger ladies-in-waiting from the next room and doled out orders quickly. In no time at all, Nadine was clean and wore a new dress, and the dirtied rug had already been replaced with a new one.

"Did you do that?" Nadine whispered to her son when they were finally alone again.

He just laughed and shook his little wooden rattle.

Before Nadine could collect her thoughts, a knock sounded at the door. Without waiting for Nadine's answer, the door burst open, and a stately woman with black and silver hair and many jewels walked in.

"Lavinia–" Nadine began, immediately moving her child to her hip. "How can I help you?" How did her mother-in-law always choose to find the worst time for everything?

"I've come for the child," the queen mother said, looking Nadine up and down. As always, Nadine suddenly felt quite shabby.

"Whatever for?" she asked, trying not to sound flustered as Rolf began chewing on her lace collar.

"You had a fall," Lavinia said evenly. "I have come to take him so you can rest."

"Oh....oh, that's quite sweet of you. Very thoughtful indeed. But I'm well enough, thank you. I had just been sitting too long, and I stood too quickly."

"I told my son you weren't the hardiest of stock," Lavina said coolly. "Come, give him here. Albert is in a meeting and needn't hear of this." She held out her arms just as Rolf had done to Nadine an hour before.

"I thank you," Nadine said, thinking quickly. "But I shall keep him with me. In fact, we'll be going to his wet nurse soon, and I promised him we would stop by the menagerie on the way."

"What, and touch those filthy animals?" the queen mother looked appalled. "Really, Nadine, have some sense."

Nadine hesitated. She was in dangerous waters here. Albert doted on both his wife and his son. But he was as dutiful to his mother as any son had ever been. And he valued her opinion over nearly anyone else's. Which would have been lovely if she hadn't seemed to think Nadine a peculiar girl from the outset, and determined to remind her son of this conviction every chance she got.

Nadine looked down into Rolf's deep blue eyes. He gazed back at her, his face full of trust and adoration.

She felt her will harden.

"No, I'll take him with me." She stalked toward the door. "Alicia, dear. I'm going out."

Alicia appeared with a tray of tea. But as soon as she understood what Nadine wanted, she readied herself to go outside and followed Nadine obediently, pausing only to glance between Nadine and her mother-in-law once before shutting the door behind her. Nadine felt as though she could still feel her mother-in-law's razor sharp gaze through the door.

"Your Highness," Alicia whispered as soon as they were in the menagerie. "Is there any way I can be of assistance?"

Nadine was about to respond with a no, but then she stopped. It was undeniable now that the faerie had gifted her son–cursed was more like it–to receive anything he wished. She'd wondered several times before when he had pointed and uttered a gurgled word here or there, but this morning, his word had been clear and commanding.

This was a nightmare.

Even the mere consideration of what his life would be like was enough to make her feel dizzy. Albert, while mercifully a good king, was already used to getting his way. And he didn't get even half the things he wished for. How was her son supposed to survive his early years? His childhood? His adolescence, getting everything he ever desired? Such evil would kill the boy, and possibly a good deal of those around him.

What had the faerie been *thinking*?

No, if she was going to give Rolf any semblance of a balanced life, Nadine would need help. She would need to shelter her son. Protect him from himself. Teach him self-control before he learned the hard way and got many others killed and injured in the process.

"Alicia," Nadine whispered. "I need you to listen fast. I have something terrible to tell you, but if you don't help me, I don't know who can."

She quickly related what happened with the faerie and her promise of the gift. When Alicia heard of Nadine's revelations, her face turned white, and her hands shook.

"Oh...Oh, Your Highness! I don't even know what to say!"

"Say you'll help me keep this a secret!" Nadine shifted Rolf to her other hip, where he pointed at a cage.

"Mine!"

Immediately, a speckled blue egg flew into his hands, leaving the offended bird furious and Alicia's mouth hanging wide open.

"Only consider," Nadine whispered fearfully as she plucked the egg out of his hands, "what that kind of power would do to a child!" She paused. "Or a king."

Alicia stood taller. "Of course, Your Highness." Her gaze, suddenly unsure, moved to the baby.

"Don't blame him," Nadine said sharply. "It's not his fault the faerie has a personal vendetta against his family."

Alicia sighed and nodded. "Of course, Your Highness. Now, we'd best get him to the wet nurse before he demands her out here."

Nadine burst into a fit of nervous giggles as she imagined the poor woman appearing in the pigpen.

"Let's go," she nodded at the path. "Now."

NADINE BLESSED Alicia in her prayers daily after that. After scheming late into the night, they decided that keeping the child as secluded as possible and giving him a simple life would be the best path forward. But to do this, as the king was greatly fond of seeing his son paraded about the court, they had to devise a story that Nadine hated intensely.

But, she reminded herself, if they didn't do something to curb the luxurious appetite that a life in court would create, people would most certainly die. So using the excuse Nadine had invoked several times already, they managed to convince the palace that the boy was indeed in very delicate health.

"He doesn't look delicate to me," Albert said one night, frowning at the little boy in his sleep.

"It's a very unusual illness," Nadine said quickly. "He cannot fight against the usual sicknesses that plague most people. He's healthy enough on his own, but should he be taken by the ague or a heavy cough or such..." She fixed her eyes on her husband, willing them to look frightened. "We may not have an heir to pass the kingdom to." She hurried to his side. "Let me raise him quietly with my first lady. Alicia is a most able nurse. He is weaning soon, as it is. We will strengthen him so he is fit to take the throne when he is ready." She forced a smile. "Go. Reassure our kingdom that he is well looked after. Alicia and I both have extensive educations. We can teach him what he needs to know for now. And when he is older, you can tell him what he needs to know about running a kingdom."

If Rolf had no self-control by the time he was a young man, Nadine doubted there would ever be hope for him.

The king studied her severely for a long moment. But then his face softened, and he touched her face. "I accused you once of not doing your duty for your people. But you give so much now, forfeiting your luxuries so that he may be well." He bent to gently kiss her lips. "I thank you."

Nadine nearly fainted from relief once the door was closed behind him.

In order to protect the prince's delicate health, Nadine and Alicia were built a cozy little cottage on the far side of the palace lawn.

And Nadine had never been happier. Alicia was a good woman, and though she was noble by birth, she was a hard worker and never once complained about how she had been yanked from the very life she'd been raised for. The three of them lived simply, passing the days in their little personal garden, which was hedged by tall bushes, and teaching the boy as he grew. Everything they could need was delivered to them without fail, and though his mother was forced to claim otherwise, Rolf grew into a strong, beautiful little boy with sun-kissed skin, dark curls, and bright blue eyes like his father. And though he did demand things as much as any child at the age of two, he wasn't unyielding to his mother's exhortations, and by the time he was four, he was really quite gentle and sweet.

While the court stayed away, upon royal edict, The king visited them often, and though she was still leery, Nadine found the times when her little family was alone together to be everything she had ever dreamed of in life. She hoped they could stay that way for a long time.

Three days before Rolf's sixth birthday, however, all of that changed.

"Nadine," the king said. "I have made a decision."

"Oh?" Nadine asked, keeping her eyes on her embroidery. It was a lazy spring evening, and their little family was enjoying one last evening in the garden before the mosquitoes came out in full.

"I've been watching Rolf, and it's come to my attention that he really is a strong boy."

Nadine looked up. "I never said he wasn't."

"You did. It's why you asked to live out here."

"I mean, he is strong," Nadine said, putting down her needlework, "but what I meant was that if he got sick, he would fare quite poorly. I never meant that his arms and legs were—"

"What *I* mean to say is that we're going to give him a proper birthday celebration."

Nadine felt the blood drain from her face. "You mean...in court?"

"Where else?" Albert stood and motioned for the boy to join them. Rolf leaped joyfully into his father's arms.

"Would you like a big birthday party?" Albert asked his son, tickling him. Rolf giggled.

"I have a party every year."

"That's right," Nadine said, trying to smile. "And you love it. We get a little cake for you, and Aunt Alicia and your father and I give you presents—"

"Who wants a little cake when he can have a monstrous cake?" the king boomed.

"A cake that looks like a monster?" Rolf's blue eyes grew wide.

"A cake as big as a monster," Albert said, his eyes bright.

"But..." Nadine stuttered. "Those people. All those people. There's surely someone who will be sick and give him–"

"He can't stay cooped up in here forever," Albert said, putting the boy down. "And before you protest too much, I'm not insisting you move him back into the palace. We'll keep everyone back in their own places. Then Rolf can come up on his own beside us." He frowned thoughtfully at the boy. "He's going to be king one day, Nadine. We can't protect him forever."

Nadine continued to protest and object for half an hour more, but eventually, the king grew cross with her, and when he left, it was not cordially.

"I've already ordered the kitchen to begin preparations," he said. "The gifts have been purchased. The court has been invited. He's attending his own birthday, and that's that!"

Nadine hardly slept for the next three days. All she could think about was the curse.

Thus far, Rolf's desires had been simple. He didn't know enough of the outside world to realize that there was more to life than what they had now. When he wanted something, it was usually something easily given or exchanged. His world was relegated to the garden, which was walled in by thick, tall topiaries. He had toys, but not overly many, and while his food was good, it wasn't too sweet or too rich. He didn't know what more there was to want.

But court...

Nadine's stomach turned at the thought of it.

Tuilidad was one of the richest kingdoms in the land. The very floor and ceilings were decked in splendor. The people were clothed in fine silks and jewels. The presents his subjects would give him would be lavish. Worst of all, however, would be the realization that there was more to the world than what he knew. And once he was aware of the magnificence of the life he would eventually lead, there would be no more going back. It was unlikely Nadine would be able to turn him away from its siren calls again.

She shivered as she imagined what he might desire when he was older and began to realize not only the draw to wealth and fame and fortune...but women as well. What if he wished for the affection of a girl when he was still too young? Would she be forced to give her heart to him against her will? Nadine was sure that she would. What if he decided he wished to marry not one, but two or three wives? What if he wanted the wife of another man?

It wasn't until late the night of the party that Nadine decided what to do.

She would tell him to wish them far away. Then, when they were out of her husband's reach, he could wish for them everything they needed to thrive. A hidden cottage. Food. Clothes, books, toys, and everything else. She and Alicia could truly raise him in secret. Then, when he was of age and properly prepared for the world, he could wish them back. And if the king wished to kill her for such a disappearance? Her son could save her from that as well.

Nadine meant to get started right away. But she had been without sleep for too long, and her frenzied thoughts wove themselves into anxious dreams as she tried to think of what she might need to do to carry her plan out. And before she knew she had fallen asleep, she was awakened by Alicia.

"It's time to wake, Your Highness," Alicia said somewhat apologetically. "The king has already come for the prince."

Nadine froze. "Rolf...Rolf is gone?"

Alicia blinked at her in surprise. "Only the castle, Your Highness." She handed Nadine a cup of tea. "There, you've been without sleep for too long. Drink this, and you'll feel good as new. She laughed a little, though it wasn't a happy laugh. "It's probably best to get you dressed and to the palace. It won't do to have the boy showing the world what he can do."

These words spurred Nadine out of bed. She was ready as fast as Alicia could make her. But it had been years since Nadine had been to a real party, and servants had to make several trips to the castle to get the baubles Alicia believed the king would deem proper for the queen to wear to a party.

Eternity seemed to pass before Nadine was reunited with her son again. By the time she found him, much to her annoyance, her mother-in-law had dressed him in a little blue tunic laced with silver buttons and a little blue cape. His trousers were black, but the boots on his feet had also been laced with silver thread. His eyes were as wide as coins as he looked about the castle at the magnificence that surrounded him.

"He looks like a true prince," the king said, beaming down at his son. "Ready to take the crown now."

"He does indeed," Lavinia said with a smug smile.

"Take the crown?" Rolf asked.

"My boy," the king said, waving his hands at the opulence surrounding them. "One day, all of this will be yours."

Rolf looked at his mother, and to her relief, seemed just as puzzled as ever.

Someone claimed the king's attention, and for a moment, both Albert and his mother were diverted.

Long enough for Rolf to notice the cake.

The cake was a monstrosity, just as the king had promised it would be. Six tiers high and piled with white frosting, a delicacy most people in their kingdom, wealthy as it was, would never even glimpse, it towered from its own table in the middle of the throne room. Rolf walked slowly over to where the castle baker, a heavy-set man with big muscles and quick hands, was smoothing the icing on the far side of the cake.

And before Nadine could stop him, Rolf looked up at the cake in delight and said softly, "I wish I had some of that cake right now."

The baker, unfortunately, had been close enough to hear Rolf's words. He gaped as a bowl appeared in the boy's hands, and a piece of cake carved itself from the largest tier. The piece of cake then plopped itself, along with a spoon, into Rolf's bowl, and Rold happily lifted it to his face.

"Rolf! No!" Nadine hissed.

Rolf, who had the bite halfway to his mouth, looked up at his mother.

"Not yet!" Nadine whispered urgently as she made it to his side. "We have to wait for the other guests!"

"Oh." Rolf looked disappointed. He stared long and hard at the cake in his hands, but then, like the sweet little boy Nadine knew so well, whispered sadly, "I wish the cake was whole again."

The slice of cake flew back up into the place from where it had been magically carved, and the bowl and spoon disappeared from Rolf's hands.

"Where's Rolf?" Nadine heard the king ask his mother.

Nadine looked once more at the baker, who still stood as though frozen in place. But he must have read the terror in her gaze, because he managed to give her a small smile and put his finger to his lips. He returned to fussing over the cake as the king made his way over to them.

Nadine nearly fainted with relief.

"What were you doing?" he asked Rolf. "Did I see a piece of cake in your hands?" He looked up in confusion at the cake.

"That...that was my fault, Your Majesty," the baker said, hurrying forward and dropping into a rushed bow. "I had some leftovers that I baked to taste, and I allowed him a bite before whisking it away."

"Oh." The king frowned down at Rolf. Then, upon meeting the boy's anxious gaze, he smiled. "Was it good?"

Nadine forced a laugh and put her hands on Rolf's

shoulders. "He's not used to such rich food. I told him not to eat much so his stomach doesn't ache."

The king still looked confused, but his attention was drawn away again after that, and while he was distracted, Nadine mouthed a silent *thank you* to the baker, who returned it with a warm smile and a wink.

CHAPTER

FOUR

The party was torture. Nadine watched miserably as Rolf's eyes were opened to all the delights of the world he hadn't known existed.

"You couldn't hide him forever," Alicia said quietly as they watched one of the courtiers present Rolf with a jeweled ball.

"No. But I had hoped to introduce him to them slowly and in good measure." Nadine sighed. She painted a bright smile on her face and nodded as Rolf turned to her and held the ball up in awe. "I wished to teach him how to handle such beautiful things. How to content himself with little and without need of the excess."

The court smiled and applauded as the boy was gifted yet a third little sword, this one encrusted with emeralds.

The king, much to Nadine's relief, seemed to have put the cake incident out of his mind. For when it was time to eat, Rolf had three pieces, and Albert laughed at his delight with each.

"He'll get sick," Alicia murmured. "Of course, I suppose that's not a problem when you can wish the stomachache away."

"Unfortunately, the solution is worse than the problem." Nadine frowned. "He'll learn he can wish the consequences away from himself at each turn."

Only as dusk was falling was the party disbanded, and the king handed a very tired Rolf to the guard tasked with carrying him home.

"You're going straight home?" the queen mother asked in her bored, nasally tone.

"Where else would I go?" Nadine asked innocently.

"Home, I hope," the king said, studying her with a slight frown. "We have a new lion, and I'm told he's not been taming well."

Nadine dropped a curtsey and led her little party outside when a sudden flower of rebellion bloomed inside her.

"Let us go to the menagerie," she said as soon as they were outside. "I wish to show my son some of the animals."

"Nadine," Alicia whispered. "I thought--"

"We won't go near the large animal enclosures," Nadine whispered back. "They're on the opposite side. I only need some space to think."

Alicia pursed her lips, and the guard looked confused and glanced back at the castle behind him once. But when pressed, he did as Nadine said. Once they were in the enclosure and settled beside a little pond where the ducks played, Nadine dismissed him.

"Don't you wish for me to remain so I can carry him for you?" the guard asked, clearly uncomfortable with abandoning his charges.

"Not at all," Nadine said, hoping her smile was sweet and disarming. "This is the perfect place for him to rest. And after I awaken him, he shall walk to the cottage." She paused. "He was near far too many people today. I wish for him to remain healthy. Fresh air will help clear out his lungs."

"Of course, Your Highness. I shall remain outside the menagerie gate, however, should you wish for me."

Nadine thanked the young man and sent him off. Once he was outside the menagerie gate, she sank down onto the grass not far from Rolf, rubbed her eyes, and then leaned back against a tree. The palace garden, which was just on the other side of the little gate, blew in the clean smells of herbs and flowers, and Nadine inhaled deeply in an attempt to calm herself.

"I'll get you some tea, Your Highness," Alicia said, already on the way to the gate.

Nadine thanked her gratefully, knowing that Alicia was one of the few people who understood her great need sometimes to be alone. Closing her eyes, she listened to the sound of the boy's breathing and tried to make her own mirror his.

Her plan from last night wouldn't work anymore. The boy now knew what he was missing, and the moment he had the inclination, he could wish himself back. And if he was in a terrible temper, as all children are from time to time, he could do what no other child could do. He could leave her behind.

Not that he had tempers often, but Nadine had been wished across the house often when he was a toddler, and she had no doubt he would think of more ways to make bigger mischief as he grew older. And in the span of a day, his world--and opportunity for mischief--had broadened exponentially.

How did one protect the boy from himself?

How did one protect the world from the boy?

Nadine's anxiety gave way to exhaustion, and her heart had finally slowed to a normal rate when she heard footsteps in the grass beside her.

"What kind of tea is it?" she called out to Alicia without opening her eyes. When Alicia didn't answer, however, Nadine looked up to see a large cloud of sparkling purple dust released over her head.

FIVE

Rolf woke up to the sound of a soft thud. He pushed himself up onto his elbows in confusion in time to see his mother collapse sideways onto the grass. A shower of purple dust covered her body, but even as he watched, it began to disappear.

"Mother!" he cried, jumping up to go to her. She was farther away from him than he'd thought when he'd lain down. He fell onto his knees at her side and put his hand on her face like he often did to wake her up at home. "Mother, wake up. Mother, stop sleeping."

His mother didn't respond.

Rolf's heart began to pound fast and hard. Forgotten were all the presents and the cake, the party, and even his time with his father. He began to shake his mother's shoulder. "Mother, please! Please wake up! Please!" He traced the shape of her face, her lovely soft face, panicked sobs beginning to choke his words. "Get up, mother! Please wake up!"

Footsteps thundered behind him, and large, meaty hands grabbed him from behind. Rolf screamed again and tried to beat at the hands with his fists, but a familiar voice whispered in his ear,

"Please, Sire! It's not safe here! We need to get you safe!"

A shout sounded from the other side of the fence.

"Quickly!" the man pleaded. "They're almost here! Now wish us to a forest! A safe forest where they can't find us!"

"I want my mother!" Rolf sobbed, now recognizing the stranger as the man who had baked his birthday cake.

"Do it!" the baker whispered, throwing a terrified glance over his shoulder. "She's very weak! But if we don't go now, the wicked faeries will hurt her more!"

Rolf stopped fighting and turned to stare at the man. Wicked faeries? Were they the ones who put the purple dust on her? Did they make her sleep?

"They want to hurt her more?" he whispered. But why would faeries want to hurt his mother? She hadn't done anything–

"Wish us to a safe forest far away!" the baker cried. "Or they will hurt her again!"

"I...I wish we were in a safe forest far away," the boy whispered. Immediately, the world around them began to melt away into a mist. But even as the old disappeared, a new one took shape. Then, in another moment, the mist was gone, and they were deep in a forest of towering trees and thick, soft undergrowth.

"I want my mother!" Rolf howled. "You said it would save her!"

The man, who had let go of him by now, looked down at him, a strange expression on his face. "My dear boy. You didn't see just as we disappeared?"

Rolf stared up at him. "See what?"

The man sighed. "The faeries put more dust on your mother. Your mother is dead."

Dead.

Dead?

Rolf's little dog had died the year before. It had been a terrible accident, one Rolf had not been able to wish undone. The little dog had eaten a flower in the garden, an orange one that had grown up near the foot of Rolf's favorite tree. Within hours, the puppy had lain down and died.

Death, his mother had explained, was when someone's body didn't move or breathe anymore. The dog's bright eyes would never open again, and though the dog looked as though she were sleeping, Rolf's mother had explained that she would never wake up. And his mother had been right. No amount of wishing had brought the dog back from the dead.

Rolf recalled her still form now as a new feeling overtook him. Anger, hot and boiling, rumbled up inside of him, and he flew into the kind of tantrum his mother had always told him he must never do.

But his mother wasn't here now to tell him to stop. And he was more afraid than he had ever been.

"I want my mother back from the dead! I want her alive again! She can't be dead! She can't!" His muscles felt all strange and tingly as he stamped his feet and screamed at the big man. "My mother isn't dead! I don't *want* her dead!"

But, as with his dog, no matter how much he kicked and screamed, no matter how he sobbed and pleaded and wished, his mother did not appear before him. She did not come back from the dead.

CHAPTER
SIX

"Would you let me explain?" the big man shouted over Rolf's screams. "Because if you don't, more people will die!"

Rolf did not let him explain. Rolf did not want to hear any more from this baker who had tricked him into wishing them away from his mother.

"I wish I was with—" Rolf began, but the big man interrupted him by covering Rolf's mouth firmly with his large, calloused hand.

"Your father will die, too!"

Rolf didn't finish his wish. He stopped screaming. He stared at the big man in horror.

"Yes!" the man said, nodding his head emphatically. "The wicked faeries are jealous of your gift! They want their magic back! You must stay hidden, or they will do bad things to your father to make you listen to them!"

"I will *wish* the bad faeries away!" Rolf stomped his foot.

"Ah, I'm afraid your wishing won't work on faeries," the big man said sadly. "For a good faerie is the one who gave you your gift. And the other faeries were jealous that she had given such a good gift to a small human boy. They wish to make you do terrible things to your father as punishment. So we must stay here so they can't catch you!"

"I wouldn't listen to them!" Rolf argued, but this time, without as much conviction.

"They would hurt your father if you didn't listen," the big man said sadly. "And all those people you met today who gave you presents."

Rolf began to shake. He shook until the big man gently lifted him and sat him on a large rock.

Why hadn't his mother told him that the bad faeries wanted him? But maybe...maybe she hadn't known. After all, the faeries had caught her by surprise.

"Why now?" Rolf whispered. "Why did the faeries come now?"

"Oh, they've always been there," the big man said mournfully. "But you've been hidden away. You haven't seen the danger your father's people live in day in and day out. Everyone in the palace is well-hidden." He pointed to Rolf. "Especially you."

"But why did they find me now?" he whimpered.

"Do you remember the cake?" the man asked gently. "And how you wished for it this morning?"

Cold and hot shame made Rolf's face prickle as he remembered. He remembered all too well. His mother had warned him not to use his wishing gift in front of other people. They wouldn't understand, she had said. But the moment Rolf had seen that beautiful cake, he'd forgotten. It was there, and it was his, waiting to be eaten.

It was because of him that his mother was dead.

Rolf began shaking even harder.

"Maybe you wouldn't be so cold," the big man said gently, "if you wished us a nice warm house. You could wish up a wonderful room for you in it, too!" Then he snapped his fingers, and his eyes lit up. "You could even wish all your birthday presents here! That way you have lots to play with! And a warm bed. And blankets and pillows and all the wonderful things that would make you feel safe and warm in your bed."

Rolf thought about this. Then a spark of hope burned in his heart. "What about Auntie Alicia? I should wish for her—"

"Oh, no! Not her." The big man shook his head. "No, the faeries can't find you here, but they could follow her. They know about her! And they could kill her, too."

Tears welled up in Rolf's eyes again. He had wanted Auntie Alicia so much. He loved her almost as dearly as his own parents. She was stern but sweet, and she gave wonderful snuggles before bed. What he liked best was when she put him on her lap, and they rocked in front of the fire, listening to its snapping and crackling as he grew tired.

"You're so cold," the big man said again. "Wish up whatever house would make you happy." His eyes twinkled. "You could wish up a castle of your very own!"

Rolf didn't want to wish up his own castle. He wanted to

wish himself away, back to his home and his father and Auntie Alicia. But he couldn't do that if the bad faeries were going to hurt them. He didn't want them to die the way his mother had died. The thought made him start to cry again.

"Your mother wouldn't have wanted you to be cold, would she?" the big man asked. "Or your father? You should do what would make them smile. You should wish up whatever will bring you happiness here."

Rolf still didn't want to do that. But he was growing very tired. His stomach hurt from eating too much cake, and what he hoped for most in the world was that he would wake up, and this whole day would be one horrible dream. His mother would be there beside him, touching his face and murmuring to him that everything would be all right, and Auntie Alicia would be standing beside her, holding a drink of water.

Yes. It must be a dream. Life couldn't be so horrible as this.

Well, in that case, he would sleep better if he had a house. So he stood and wished for a house. It was actually his own house, the cottage he had slept in at home. The cottage was smaller than the big man liked at first, and Rolf was instructed several times to make improvements.

At first, Rolf listened, but eventually, he started for the door. "I'm going in. And I'm going to bed."

The big man stopped telling him what to change and immediately agreed that that would be best. Rolf found his room quickly and, though he knew he'd wished them there, was quite relieved to see not only his birthday presents but

54

his other favorite toys as well. And there was his bed and his rug, and even the little stuffed dog his mother had sewn for him for his second birthday.

Rolf went straight to his bed and crawled inside. He breathed deeply, smelling the scent of his mother, where she often lay beside him to help him sleep.

"I wish her smell would stay here forever," he whispered as he scrambled beneath his sheets and huddled there, clutching his toy dog to his chest.

"This is...quite plain," the big man said, looking around the room.

"It's my home," Rolf whimpered.

The big man looked at him again, and his eyes softened. "Of course it is. Now, before you go to sleep, I have one more thing I must ask you to wish for."

"What is it?" Rolf frowned at him. He was getting a little tired of all the big man's wishes.

"My brother stayed behind this evening to look for the bad faeries to see if they discovered where we went." The big man knelt beside the bed, getting his dirty boots all over Rolf's rug. His mother never would have allowed that.

"Please wish him here so that he can tell us whether the bad faeries are still at your father's castle or if they have gone away." He paused. "So we know your father and your..."

"Auntie Alicia."

"Yes, that your Auntie Alicia is safe."

Rolf hesitated. That seemed reasonable enough, so he nodded. "I wish the big..." He paused. "What's your name?"

"Oh, um, you can call me Tobias. And my brother's name is Josif."

Rolf nodded. "I wish that Tobias's brother, Josif, was here." As the words left his mouth, another figure, surrounded by white smoke, began to materialize in his room. A taller, thinner version of Tobias blinked up at them.

"What just—"

"His Royal Highness, Prince Rolf," Tobias said in an overly loud voice, "brought you so that you may tell us if the bad faeries have left his father's castle."

Josif blinked at him several times before nodding vigorously. "Oh, yes. 'f course." He bowed. "Prince Rolf, Th', 'um, bad faeries're gone." He glanced at Tobias, who for some reason, glared at him.

"And Auntie Alicia?" Rolf pressed.

"Um, oh. Yes. She's fine, too."

Rolf didn't think much of the man's brains. He seemed far too confused for Rolf's taste. But Rolf was glad to hear his father and Auntie Alicia were safe. Now he could go to sleep, and in the morning, he would wake up and find that it was just a dream.

CHAPTER
SEVEN

To My Dear Mother,

Forgive my lack of opening pleasantries, but did you hear? Nadine has been arrested!

Apparently, she took the prince into the menagerie after his birthday party even though the king told her not to, and it seems they were attacked by a wild animal. There was blood all over the place. The boy was so mangled that they never even found his entire body. It was all counted as an accident until certain letters were discovered in Nadine's cottage that she had meant to send to a friend, wherein she lamented the constant attention the boy required and wished very much to be free of her charge.

The guards and bailiffs were all very much unsure what to make of it. The queen mother wanted her charged with negligence, and I believe they were considering that charge *until the letters were discovered. Now there is talk of a beheading.*

Of course, this doesn't strike most of us as a surprise. She was always odd. She hated balls and parties and preferred animals to people all the time. If you had the misfortune of talking to her, she disliked looking you in the eye. And the way she talked was just...well, different. To this day, I cannot understand why the king chose her over me, or even Serah. I suppose he believed she would be a good, docile girl, which I'll admit, I'm not at all times. In this case, however, that might work in my favor.

Either way, this is what happens when you choose a wife who's not right in the head. Perhaps the king will learn his lesson this time.

That said, I wish for you to join us at my brother's manor in town as soon as the king's mourning period is over. I'm sure they'll execute her soon. The king could change things, of course, but he was never in love with her to begin with. As it was, they lived apart for nearly five years. So once the mourning period is over, the king will need a new queen, especially now that his doe-eyed brat is out of the way. Heirs are rather important like that, and I could fix his lack easily. If you help me prepare, I have little doubt that I can secure the crown after all.

Your dear son urges you to come as well. He says it's no trouble at all for you to stay in the room you had before. I can hardly wait.

Love,

Chrysanthemum

CHAPTER
EIGHT

R olf stared sadly at the ball in front of him. It wasn't the new jeweled ball he'd received for his birthday. This ball, with its brown leather and stitches, was the one his mother had presented him with on his last birthday.

It felt like a long time since his mother died. And though Tobias said it had only been seven weeks, Rolf felt like those seven weeks had lasted longer than he'd been alive. Every day felt the same. There were no morning kisses and snuggles. Breakfast, of course, was whatever Rolf wanted, but it wasn't the same as when Auntie Alicia tucked a napkin into his shirt and said grace with him and his mother. There was no reading practice in his mother's lap. No writing practice with Auntie Alicia. No playing ball with his father in the garden. No stories nor snuggles good night.

Going to sleep was the hardest. Rolf had always gone to sleep with his mother close by. Even if she wasn't in the room, which was often, he'd known she was near. He could hear her low conversations with Auntie Alicia, or the sound of her soft snores coming from her bed. Now the bed was always cold because his mother never came to sit or lie next to him, and he'd taken to huddling with his little stuffed dog, pretending he just couldn't feel her but that she was still there. For a few days, he'd wished that the bed was warm as if she was there, but for some reason, that was even worse than when it was cold.

And now, when he eventually did get to sleep, usually after hours of sobbing himself to exhaustion, he had dreams which shook him to the core. Dreams where his mother died over and over again. And when he awoke, shaking and drenched with sweat, he would wish those dreams away only to have new terrors haunt his sleep at night.

"That's it!" Tobias stormed out of the house to the little clearing where Rolf sat on his favorite stump. "I've had it with this moping! Every time I go to work, you're staring. And every time I come back, you're doing nothing."

Rolf turned to glare at him. He'd wished a traveling coin into existence for the baker so he could go to work and come back whenever he wanted without Rolf having to wish it for him. He had to keep an eye on the king to see if the wicked faeries came back, he had told Rolf. And to Rolf, that had made sense.

Still, while Tobias might be keeping him safe, Rolf would remember this the next time Tobias wanted a new room added onto the already sprawling house. See if he got what he wanted then. In fact, Rolf was tempted to wish some sort of yucky creature onto Tobias's bossy head. Then the big man could see how he liked that for a change.

Tobias paused when he met Rolf's glare. "What I mean to say," his voice was suddenly pleasant, "is that you should wish up a friend for yourself. Someone to live here with you and to play with."

Rolf opened his mouth to wish a giant octopus onto the man's head, the kind he'd read about in one of his mother's books, but then he stopped. Actually...

A friend might not be so bad.

"Yes!" Tobias added quickly, his words rushed. "A little girl, perhaps!"

Rolf considered this. He'd never had a friend before. Not outside of his mother, Auntie Alicia, and his father. But he'd read about them in books. And in those books, the characters had seemed to like having friends.

"But..." he said slowly, "you said we can't tell anyone we're here. Or the wicked faeries will find us."

"Oh, I don't mean from the castle! Instead, think about the kind of little girl you'd like to play with." Tobias squatted beside Rolf, his eyes bright the way they were whenever he had a new idea. "One who likes to play ball, for instance? Or one who tells good stories. And probably about your age. You could build her a lovely little room! She could tell you all the things she wanted, and you could make her very happy!"

Rolf looked back at the house. It was now far bigger than it had been when he'd first wished it here. Tobias kept thinking of things they might need that Rolf ought to wish for. There was a room with a large store of gold coins in it, and another that held enough food to feed an army. Tobias had also realized he would need a great many clothes so he could dress differently and sneak into the court often to hear anything the people in the king's court might be saying about the wicked faeries. To do that, he insisted, he would need a great number of different suits so no one would recognize him. He needed to wear lots of jewels as well. Then, of course, there was the room for his brother, Josif, who hardly ever ventured out after it had been built.

Another room for a girl wouldn't be a problem. Only... did a little girl want to come live with him?

"What if she doesn't *want* to come?" he asked Tobias slowly. "What if she wants to stay where she is?"

"Oh, but you'll be helping her!" Tobias exclaimed, dropping to one knee. "Think of how you're saving her from the wicked faeries as well!"

Rolf stared at him. "But...I thought they were only looking for me."

Tobias scoffed. "Do you think you're the only little boy the faeries wish to trouble? Children are small and useful. Many faeries have taken little children just for the fun of it! And now that you're gone, and they can't get your magic back, they're angry!" He dropped his voice. "Only two days ago, I heard that a whole family of children was taken."

"I hadn't thought of that." Rolf frowned at a nearby rock. "But if the faeries are going around hurting the children, we should save as many children as we can–"

"Oh, no! We can't do that!" Tobias slightly paled. "Too many, and the faeries would notice! But one little girl..." He shrugged. "One little girl should be fine. And if you choose a little girl who's poor, think of all the pretty gifts and nice clothes you can give her. You'll be saving her from the wicked faeries and from poverty."

Rolf didn't know what poverty was, but he knew that he would like to help a little girl if he could. And it would be fun to use his gift to make her smile. Sometimes, he used to wish up pretty things for his mother or Auntie Alicia, and that had always made them very happy.

"Very well," he said, nodding once. "I'll do it. Only," he turned to Tobias, "I'll do it after you go."

Tobias blinked at him. "Why is that?"

"Because you're big and ugly. And you might scare her."

Tobias scowled down at Rolf as he stood. But he only turned sharply as he pulled Rolf's coin out of his pocket. "Well, then!"

"And take Josif with you!" Rolf yelled. "I don't want him scaring her either!"

Tobias's scowl deepened. "And what am I supposed to do with that vagabond while I'm at work?"

"Take. Him. Away." Rolf stood and stamped his foot.

Tobias didn't smile, but he did harrumph and make his way into the house, where he started shouting for Josif.

Once he was sure they were both gone, Rolf turned and focused on his wish. He had to be careful. His mother had warned him thus often while she was alive. And over the last few weeks, both he and Tobias had learned the hard way that the words Rolf used mattered whenever he made a wish. So now, he scrunched his eyes shut and thought hard.

"I wish...I wish I had a little girl to live here and play with me. One who likes to read and play ball and tell stories. I wish she was nice and smart like my mother. I wish she was poor so I can give her things and protect her from the wicked faeries." He paused. The magic usually gave him a few seconds to specify his requests so he could get them right. "And I wish she was here now."

White smoke began to swirl around the clearing. Then, as the smoke cleared, a small figure was left in its wake, crouching and all huddled in a ball, big blue eyes peeking up at him. She had soft brown curls and pale skin, and Rolf thought she was the most beautiful thing he had ever seen in his life.

After his mother, of course.

"Hello," he said, stepping toward her. "I'm Rolf."

CHAPTER
NINE

The girl screamed and scrambled backward, tearing her dress beneath her bare foot as she did. Her elbows buckled, and she was suddenly flat on her back.

"It's all right!" Rolf said, hurrying after her. "I can fix it!" He looked at her torn dress, which was faded and rather threadbare. "I wish her dress was fixed."

Immediately, the dress closed the hole and looked as if it had never been torn in the first place. But for some reason, this only made the girl scream more.

"It's fixed now, don't you see?" Rolf asked, kneeling beside her where she lay trembling. "It will all be well!"

"Who are you?" the girl shrieked. "Where am I? Where's my family?"

"I brought you here," Rolf said excitedly. "To save you from the wicked faeries! You're safe now!"

"What wicked faeries?" the girl cried, her voice trembling. "I want to go home! I want my mother!"

Rolf froze. He knew that feeling. He knew that fear. And suddenly, Rolf felt as though he might cry, too.

The girl got to her feet and backed up again, just to collide with a tree. But before Rolf could reach her, she turned and ran. And she was fast.

Rolf tried to follow her, but he wasn't used to running through the forest like this girl seemed to be. He'd only ever run through his garden at the cottage, and it had always been trimmed neatly by gardeners at night while he slept. Now he tripped and cut his hands and feet as he tried fruitlessly to catch her. Where was she going? Surely she didn't think she could run home. Finally, he stopped running. As soon as he caught his breath, he said,

"I wish I was with the girl, and I wish I could run through the forest like her!"

As soon as the white smoke came and cleared, Rolf was right behind the girl again. She was slowing, which made it easy for him to catch up. When she turned and looked behind her, her eyes grew wide, and she shrieked again.

"How did you get here?" She stopped running but continued to back up, which meant she tripped on a branch and hit the ground hard.

"I'm not trying to hurt you!" Rolf said, starting to feel a little angry. "I'm trying to keep you safe!"

"But you..." her eyes were as wide as walnuts. "You can wish..."

"Yes, yes. I get everything I wish for," he snapped. "It's

why the wicked faeries are after me. And it's what I'm trying to keep you safe from, too!"

She finally sat still. "But...there aren't any wicked faeries trying to get me. The only faerie we have in our village is good and kind!"

Rolf looked at the ground. "Tobias says most faeries are wicked. A good faerie gifted me, and now all the others are looking for me to take my gift away."

"Your...your gift? You mean...wishing?"

He finally looked up at her and nodded. She frowned and stood, brushing herself off. She'd gotten several more cuts as she'd run. He'd have to heal those.

"But," she continued, "if the faeries are looking for you, didn't you put me in more danger by bringing me here to you? To the person they're looking for?"

Rolf opened his mouth to answer, then stopped. That was a good question. Then he shook his head. "They can't find us. I wished it. This is the one place in the world that they can't find." He raised his arms and looked around them. If the wood they were standing in wasn't magical, it certainly looked it. The evergreen trees were so tall that they were hidden in the near constant cloud cover. Flowers of all colors populated themselves in thick colonies all over the ground, and the lichens were brilliant hues of red, blue, purple, yellow, and orange against the verdant green moss. Weak sunlight flitted in and out of the trees, casting beams of gold that burst through the clouds here and there.

"But..." the girl whimpered. "I wasn't in danger."

"You were in danger." He ducked beneath a low branch

and came to stand beside her. "You just didn't know it." He looked up at the sky, though he couldn't see much of it beyond the clouds. Just little patches of blue here and there. "They're always out there."

"Then my father will protect me!" her voice began to shake again. "Please let me go home!"

"Can your father fight faeries?" Rolf asked.

The girl frowned. "No, but–"

"See? Tobias says you'll be safer here. And he was right."

The girl's frown deepened. "Who is Tobias?"

"He's taking care of me. He saved me from the bad faeries when they killed my mother." He paused. "I wanted to save lots of children–boys and girls–from the wicked faeries by bringing them here and taking care of them. But he said I could only save one other child from the faeries, otherwise, they would notice."

"But why did you choose me?" the girl asked.

Rolf shrugged. "I just described the kind of friend I wanted to have, and the magic chose you." He gave her a little, hopeful smile. "I'm glad it did."

But the girl shook her head and stomped her foot. "*I'm* not." She turned sharply and began walking deeper into the woods.

"Where are you going?" Rolf asked.

"Home!"

"But you won't get home that way!" he called. "We're on a mountain!"

The girl froze. Then she turned slowly. "A...a mountain?"

He nodded. "You won't get home that way. But you'll

probably fall off a cliff." He shuddered. "I almost did." He'd been so sad during his first week that on the second or third day, he'd begun walking. He hadn't walked with any particular purpose. He'd just walked. And walked and walked. Until he was suddenly on a precipice, and if he hadn't been able to wish himself safe again, he would have fallen to his death.

"Come," he said, holding out his hand. "We can go to my cottage. I'll wish you a room just the way you like! And fancy clothes and sweets and anything you like!" As he spoke, he felt hope rise within him.

The girl didn't smile, though. In fact, she didn't say anything. She only glanced back longingly at the deeper forest before sighing and giving him one slight nod.

"I wish we were back at the cottage," he said, not looking away from her face.

Immediately, they found themselves stepping out of white smoke tendrils and into the clearing by the cottage. She froze and stared.

"That's a cottage?"

"Well, it *was* one." He shrugged. "But Tobias keeps asking for new rooms. Yours will go right here!" He bounded over to a spot where a window currently sat. "I wish..." Rolf paused. "What's your name?"

But the girl raised her chin and mashed her lips together. "I'm not telling unless you send me home."

Rolf stared at her, the feeling of annoyance and frustration returning. He was doing this to help her! Didn't she understand that?

"Fine," he said as he faced the cottage again. "I wish my friend had a room right here. A room with a big canopy bed, and a vanity like my mother's, and a wardrobe full of princess dresses, and lots of dolls and toys, and a big, soft braided rug. And make everything pink and white. Give her two windows, and put roses all over the room that will never get old and die." Rolf wasn't an expert on girls, but he did know the kinds of things his mother and Auntie Alicia liked.

The girl's stony expression quickly turned to one of panic as the wish started coming to fruition. She squeaked and ran to grab Rolf's arm.

"What's happening?" she whispered, squeezing him until it hurt.

"I told you. It's my gift. My wishes come true."

"But...but it's so much!"

It was indeed a big wish. The room was smaller than his, due to the size of the clearing. But it was far fancier than anything Rolf had in his room.

"Come and see!" he said, pulling her toward the kitchen door. She allowed him to lead her, her mouth still hanging wide open as they went inside. Once in the kitchen, they quickly spotted her new door, which was painted white with pink filigree dancing in intricate patterns from bottom to top. Rolf scrambled to open the door for her the way his father always did for his mother.

And as she walked inside, she let out the smallest, "Oh!"

The room was the most elegant place Rolf had ever seen besides the palace. Not that he'd seen many places. But it was far more luxurious than his own cottage had been. Of course, that was the way he wanted it. If he had to take this little girl from her family, which was bothering him more and more by the minute, she deserved to have the most beautiful room in the world.

Blue diamonds glittered in the ceiling like stars, and gems of all kinds were scattered throughout the rest of the room from the bed to the wardrobe to even her toys. Little steps led up to the bed, which was quite high and looked very soft, and vines of roses wound their way all around the edges of the walls and the posts of the bed. Dolls like those he'd seen in his mother's books covered the bed.

As if in a daze, the little girl walked slowly over to the wardrobe and opened it to find dozens of dresses like the women at his birthday party had worn, all made of silks and laces and gems sewn into them with silver and gold thread.

"Do you like it?" Rolf asked breathlessly. "I can change anything if you like! Just ask it, and I'll wish!" Then an idea hit him. "Do you like to read? I have lots of books! Mother always says–said..." he paused and had to clear his throat. "She always said most people don't have books. But I can wish you as many as you want." He felt a grin spreading across his face. "We can be friends and play and–"

The girl, who had been turning in a slow circle, finally turned to face him again. And when she did, there were tears in her eyes.

"I just want to go home."

THE GIRL DIDN'T SPEAK a word after that. Instead of climbing on her bed or trying on the dresses or looking at her toys, she'd only gone back outside and sat upon the stump Rolf often sat on out in the clearing. Pulling her skinny arms and legs up against her chest, she'd begun rocking herself slightly and hadn't moved since.

Rolf, who had settled on the stoop where he could see her, hadn't either.

It was dusk by the time Rolf felt the familiar roil of magic beside him. As expected, Tobias appeared in his own whirl of smoke behind him.

"Oh, so you listened to me, eh?" He scrunched his eyes at her. "Why's she sitting out in the dark?"

"She doesn't want to be here," Rolf said in a flat voice. "She wants to go home."

"Did you give her all the pretty things we talked about?"

"Yes."

Tobias squinted at her again. "What's wrong with her then?"

At the sound of his voice, the girl had given a slight start and turned. Then she stood and marched toward the house, a sudden fierce expression on her thin face.

"Are you Tobias?" she demanded, coming to stand in front of the big man.

Tobias was nearly twice as tall as she was, and he put his

78

fists on his hips and stared down at her. "Aye, that'd be me. And who would–"

Before he got the words out of his mouth, the girl had drawn her scrawny leg back and kicked Tobias hard in the shin.

"What? What's possessed you?" Tobias jumped back and lifted his leg to rub it.

"You've lied to him." She glowered up at him. "You told him wicked faeries are all over the world trying to take children."

"What? I mean, they are! Ow! Would you stop that?"

The girl had kicked him in the other shin. "Tell him the truth so he will send me home!"

"I'm... I'm not lying! And don't you kick me again!" He wrapped his meaty hands around her arms and looked as if he was going to pick her up, but Rolf threw himself between them.

"Don't touch her!" he shouted, delivering his own kick to Tobias's leg.

Tobias's whole face turned red, and he puffed his chest and shoulders up and took a step toward them.

"I wish you were the size of a bunny!" Rolf yelled as fast as he could.

In a burst of smoke, Tobias was gone, and Rolf had to wait for the smoke to clear to see the man, who was now barely taller than Rolf's knee, looking around in what seemed like absolute terror. Rolf reached down and picked him up with both hands the way he'd once done with his puppy when she was naughty.

"I'm glad you're protecting me," Rolf said, grinding his teeth together. "But you're not going to touch her. You're going to protect *both* of us."

"My apologies!" the big man said, holding onto Rolf's hands with his tiny ones. "I won't do it again! My leg just hurt, but I shouldn't have got angry! I'm sorry!"

"See that you are," Rolf said, glaring at the man once more before putting him down. "I wish he was his own size again."

Breaking glass sounded from the doorway. Rolf looked up to see Josif staring at them, mouth open and a broken tea cup at his feet.

"And that'll happen to you, too, if you try to hurt her!" Rolf snarled at him. Josif blinked twice before nodding and running to his room.

"Who's that?" the girl asked in a quiet voice.

"Josif, Tobias's brother. He's strange, but less bossy than this one." Rolf glared back up at Tobias.

"No insult intended," Tobias said, backing away slowly, his large hands held out in front of him. "We'll all get along just fine." Then he peeked around Rolf at the girl. "Are you sure you don't want to send her back and get a new one, though?"

The stamp of Rolf's foot made his answer clear, and Tobias hurried away, mumbling something about dinner.

"You can cook!" Rolf shouted after him. "I'm done wishing for you tonight!" He turned back to the girl. "Sorry about that." If Rolf was honest with himself, Tobias frightened him a bit, too. But he would never admit that to the big man. Tobias was the only one who had seen the faeries kill his mother. He was Rolf's only hope for figuring out how to defeat the wicked faeries. And the fact that he had just dared to shrink Tobias was making Rolf a bit dizzy.

"What would you like to eat tonight?" he asked the girl, hoping his heroic deed would make her smile.

But she was looking away. "Nothing, thank you," she whispered. Then she went and sat outside again.

CHAPTER
TEN

The week after Rolf's mother died had been bad. And though Rolf wouldn't have dreamed it possible, the week after the girl arrived was nearly just as awful.

Rolf's own suffering had briefly subsided the day the girl had come. Having someone to take care of had, for a few short moments, chased away the ever-present hole in his heart. But the girl didn't want to be taken care of. She didn't want to play or talk, and she barely ate, only picking at the food he brought her. Though she did return to her room at night when the evening cold set in, the majority of her day was spent out on the stump, staring off into the forest.

Doing exactly as Rolf had done.

And Rolf's pain felt as though it had doubled. Now there was suffering from within and without. And if he'd known she would be safe from the bad faeries...if he could just know for sure, he would send her home. This was too much sadness. He wanted to make the sadness go away. It was more than he could take.

Sometimes, Rolf became angry, yelling in his room. Throwing things. Beating his pillow and bed until they were rumpled and messy, something he would have been scolded for at home. Sometimes he hated the girl. He was saving her, and she couldn't see it. Sometimes, he wanted to hug her and tell her the pain would go away. Sometimes, he felt so numb he didn't care.

But the eighth morning after her arrival, the sun was unusually strong, chasing away many of the thick clouds that floated so close to the forest floor. And with the sun, Rolf felt a surge of hope. So he went out and stood beside her.

"Um..." He looked around, searching for anything that might be enticing. "The sun is out."

The girl just continued to stare listlessly into the trees.

"I thought...I noticed you don't wear the princess dresses. Would you like something else? I can make you anything you want."

At this, she turned and looked at him, her blue eyes rimmed with red.

"I want to go home." She sat taller, and her eyes narrowed. "You took me away, and I just want to go home!"

"I thought..."

"You're bad at thinking then! Stop asking me to play! Stop asking me if I want dresses or toys or food! Just take me home!" She'd risen from the stump, and her voice had become a shout.

Rolf's first reaction was anger. But as he opened his mouth to retort that she was ungrateful and foolish for wanting to live in a town with a faerie, a new idea struck him.

"I wish you were hap—"

"No!" Her scream was so sharp Rolf jumped. But the fury on her face was ten times what it had been that first day.

"No?" he repeated.

"I know what you were going to do! You were going to use magic on me! And don't you ever, ever use magic on me! I'm not a pet! I'm a girl! And if I can't be where I want, I should be allowed to feel what I want!"

Rolf stared at her as she came closer and closer. "I...I was only trying to help!" he stuttered.

"You're a wicked boy for bringing me here, and I'll never, ever play with you as long as you live! So if you're going to keep asking, just stop!" Her eyes were wild and wide, and she was breathing as if she'd just run a race.

Rolf's eyes stung, and he felt large tears welling in them. Angry tears. And hurt tears. Tears his mother would have wiped away.

Swiveling around, he started running. He didn't stop running until he reached his room and threw himself on his bed. And then he cried as he hadn't since the day his mother had died.

"I want to go home!" he wailed into his stuffed dog. "I just want to go home! I want everyone to go home!" For one moment, he almost wished it. But the memory of his father and Tobias's warnings about what would happen to his loved ones if Rolf went back kept his tongue from doing what it wanted most in the world to do.

"Mother!" he wailed. "Mother, come back! Mother, I need you! I need you! Please come to me! Please, Mother!"

He had nearly cried himself to sleep when he felt a hand on his shoulder. Jerking his head up, he half expected to see his mother standing there. Maybe, he had somehow wished her back from the dead!

But it wasn't his mother. Instead, it was the girl.

"What do you want?" he growled into his pillow, pulling away from her touch.

"Your mother died?" she asked in a voice so soft he could barely hear her.

"I told you she did." He glared at her. "The wicked faeries killed her. All because I used my gift where they could see me. And now she's *dead*." His voice broke on the last word, and he hid his face in the pillow again.

The bed moved beneath him. When he peeked up again, the girl had climbed up to sit beside him. She didn't say anything, but she was there. And though she had been very angry with him, and he had been angry with her, Rolf realized he felt a little better. He was still sad. His mother was still gone.

But right now...he wasn't alone.

"Do you have a portrait of your mother?" the girl finally asked.

He sniveled. "A what?"

"A portrait. A picture of her." She looked down at her hands, clasping and unclasping them. "Once, when my father had an extra gold piece, he paid a traveling artist to sketch a likeness of my mother." She smiled a little. It was the first time Rolf had seen her smile, and he decided it was a very pretty smile.

"It's my father's favorite possession. He keeps it safe in a wooden trunk, but sometimes, I see him pull it out and look at it."

Rolf considered this. He had seen several large paintings of different kings and queens in the palace. He hadn't thought of it before, as they had no portraits in the cottage. But now...

"I wish I had a portrait of my mother," he said, his wish ending with a hiccup.

A little puff of white smoke appeared on the wall beside his bed. Both children turned and watched in awe as a large golden frame appeared, so large it took up nearly that entire portion of the wall, from the bed to the ceiling. Then inside the frame, color began to appear. First in little lines and blotches, but the longer they watched, the more Rolf began to recognize the likeness within.

"She's beautiful!" the girl breathed.

Rolf nodded, his throat too tight to speak. When he felt a gentle pressure on his hand, however, he looked down to see that the girl had taken it gently in hers.

And there, with his mother smiling down at him, and his hand held for the first time in eight weeks, Rolf felt like he could breathe again for the first time.

He turned shyly to the girl. "Would...would you like a portrait of your family in your room as well?"

The girl gave him a wry grin. "I'd like to go home. But if I have to stay here for now, yes. I'd like one." She laughed a little. "Just maybe not so big as this."

For a long time, the children sat and stared at their portraits.

"Bethan," the girl finally said.

"What?" Rolf looked away from his mother to face the girl.

"My name is Bethan." She gave him another half-smile. "I just thought you should know." Then she paused and looked at the bookshelf. "You said you liked stories. Would... would you like to read one?"

Rolf felt his chest expand with joy. He nodded quickly. "I love stories. Do you?"

The girl smiled, a little wider this time. "I do." She leaned closer, and her eyes grew mischievous. "Most of the people in our village can't read. But our faerie taught me how."

"Oh." Rolf didn't know what to think of this. "I have lots of stories. My father's library is big, and he brought us lots of books. I...I wished a lot of them here." He looked at the little shelf. "You can take any you like."

The girl got up and examined the books. As she studied them, Rolf realized what he needed to do.

"I can't send you home, but...I promise to never use my magic on you. I mean, I'll use it if you fall off a cliff or something. I'll never wish you happy, though, or make you think or feel something you don't want to." He paused and swallowed. "I promise."

She studied him for a minute before giving him a wry smile. "I still think you should send me home, but... you're not a wicked boy after all."

"You can think what you want about me!" He stood. "Just as long as we can be friends." He paused once more. "And I'll send you home as soon as the wicked faeries are gone! I promise."

ELEVEN YEARS LATER...

CHAPTER
ELEVEN

Rolf proudly presented Bethan with his string of fish. "And that's one more bet in the books for me."

Bethan rolled her eyes, but Rolf didn't miss her little smile as she continued to chop onions. "It took you long enough."

"You're just jealous because now you have to make supper."

Bethan held up the knife and the onion and raised one eyebrow.

"No, tomorrow. Our bet was for who makes supper *tomorrow*." Rolf dropped the fish on the table beside where she was cutting. "And I think I want—"

Bethan let out a small shriek. "Rolf, no! Not on the table! Go clean them! And then come back and clean the table."

Tobias appeared in a puff of smoke in the far corner of the kitchen, but as soon as he saw Rolf and Bethan, he rolled his eyes. "Really, when you can wish your food into existence, I don't see why anyone would want to kill and cook it themselves."

"I like doing things for myself sometimes," Rolf said, studying with satisfaction the size of his fish. "Being utterly useless doesn't really suit my taste."

"And," Bethan added smoothly, "some of us like to have *purpose* in our lives." Her tone was cool, and she kept her eyes on her work, but from her little smile, Rolf guessed that she knew she'd succeeded in making Tobias turn red.

At least she wasn't kicking the big man the way she'd done when she was small. But for some reason, Tobias didn't seem to think her new expression of displeasure much better.

"Where's my useless brother?" he asked, scowling as he shook his coat out and hung it on the wooden peg in the corner. If it had been up to Tobias by now, they probably would have been living in a palace. But Bethan had been staunchly set against making the house too grand. And much to Tobias's chagrin, Rolf had agreed with her.

"Outside fetching me some basil from the garden," Bethan answered evenly.

"I keep him around to keep an eye on you two, and all he does is slink off by himself." Tobias shook his head and went to his room, his muttering shifting from his lazy brother to something about a domineering woman.

"And you," Bethan turned back to Rolf, flicking him with a little handful of water. "Go clean those fish. I want them ready for breading."

Rolf happily took his fish out to the little creek just behind the house and began to clean them. Tobias may not have approved of the dirty work, but Rolf really did enjoy the labor. Wishing, as Bethan liked to point out, had nothing to do with *him* or his abilities. It all came from the faerie's magic. Rolf liked putting some of himself out into the world sometimes just to know he could.

When he was twelve, he'd wished into existence a book with pictures to show him how to do whatever he asked. He'd learned all kinds of useful skills, such as setting traps for hares, cutting firewood, using a crossbow, and catching and cleaning fish. He had to, of course, wish many of the tools into existence, as there was no one nearby from which he could buy them. And even though these book-learned skills never quite filled the hole that seemed to exist permanently inside of him, the one deep down that told him he was nothing more than a lost, spoiled prince, they helped dull the ache.

And today, that ache was a little duller than usual. Hopefully, in fact, today would change everything.

He washed his hands in the creek and brought the fish back to the kitchen before sneaking up into his room.

It was still much as it had been when he'd first arrived, though he had several new areas he'd created in what had once been clean, empty corners. In the northwest corner stood his wood-carving table, which always seemed covered in wood shavings no matter how often he wished it cleaned up. His southwest corner was filled with bookshelves to keep all the books he and Bethan had wished up over the years to learn and keep them occupied.

Now, he went to one of his bookshelves and carefully drew out his latest creation. His heart bounced up and down in his chest as he looked over it one more time. He knew she would love it. She loved anything he made for her. But, as always, the voice in his head whispered that it could never make up for him taking her from her family.

No, it could never do that.

But it was the best he could do. And as long as he was taking care of her, he was going to take care of her the best that he knew how. Because Bethan deserved everything he could give. His heart seemed to jump even higher into his throat as he thought of what that might mean for both of them tonight.

"It occurs to me," he announced as he returned to the kitchen, "that you ought to be cooking tonight, Tobias."

Tobias, who must have returned to the kitchen while Rolf was in his room, stared at him. "Why would I do that?"

"Because it happens to be Bethan's birthday."

Bethan paused her work, coating the fish in bread-crumbs and herbs, and beamed at him. "You remembered!"

"Of course, I remembered." He pulled the book from behind his back. "I've been working on this." He held it out and grinned. "Here's your first present."

Bethan's eyes grew wide, and she dropped her utensils and walked slowly up to Rolf, wiping her hands on her apron. "You...you made me a book?"

Rolf nodded as she stared, open-mouthed, at his

creation. With one finger, she reached out and gently stroked the thin wooden cover.

"It's heavy," Rolf said, feeling like he might just burst with pride. Her reaction was everything he'd hoped for and more. "The front, back, and spine are actual wood. You wouldn't believe how many pieces I broke before I got them as thin as I wanted. And the pages are bound to the spine and covers with leather." His voice caught in his throat, as he realized she was still staring at it. "Do...do you like it?"

"Rolf! I can't even... It's breathtaking!" she whispered.

Her fingers traced the image he'd carved into the front cover, a moon and sun and stars over a forest. He wouldn't admit it to her for the world, but this particular skill had only been possible to hone with the help of a few wishes after his book had been unable to teach him some of the finer parts of the craft. But wishes or no, the work itself was all his.

"Open it!" he urged her.

She lifted the cover and laughed. But it wasn't a derisive laugh. It was the one he loved, where her voice tinkled like the little bell she kept on her pet rabbit he'd given her last year. "It's a portrait!" she cried. "Of us!"

He nodded. "That was the day we found the wild blackberries."

"Before we got into poison oak," she added dryly.

He waved his hand. "It was only a few minutes of misery. I wished it all away as soon as we broke out in rashes."

She shook her head but laughed again before turning the page.

Tobias had to remind them twice that supper wasn't done before she returned to her work. While she did, though, Rolf continued to turn the pages so she could see the portraits he'd wished up, recalling their days together over the last eleven years. As they laughed and talked, though, Rold found focusing more and more difficult, as often happened these days. Bethan was just so beautiful.

If she had seen herself in the mirror he'd gifted her three years ago, she would have said she was a mess. Her brown curls were mostly pulled up on the back of her head, but several locks had made their way down and hung loosely around her face. There were crumbs sticking to her apron, and her feet were dirty, as she preferred to walk around barefoot, despite his many gifts of proper shoes. She wore one of her working dresses, the plain kind she insisted on sewing for herself, as her mother had taught her to sew, and her hands were covered in fish, eggs, and breadcrumbs.

But what he was sure she didn't see were the graceful lines of her jaw, or the way her eyes burned brightly like the morning star. She didn't see how pretty her ankles were, or the way her body had begun to curve over the last few years. Her lips looked soft and pink, and he wanted very much to know what they felt like.

He knew, however, without a doubt that mentioning such things would get him into trouble as they had before. But he was going to change all of that tonight. They were both seventeen now, as he'd had his birthday three months before. According to Josif, in Rolf's homeland, both he and Bethan were both of age. And Rolf had read enough books to know what that meant.

Supper was boisterous and loud, with even Josif shyly chiming in about the portraits they continued to reminisce over, his quiet voice adding details to memories neither Rolf nor Bethan remembered. Only Tobias sat in silence, glowering at his plate as they ate. Still, to Rolf, the meal seemed to drag on forever. He couldn't wait until they were free to take the evening stroll they often did after supper. But just as he began to push his chair back, his heart suddenly pounding throughout his entire body once more, Tobias clapped him on the shoulder.

"Talk with me," he said in a low voice as Bethan stood and began to gather the dishes. He nodded at the door.

"Tomorrow," Rolf said as he pushed his chair in. "Tonight, I have another birthday surprise for Bethan."

"No. We're talking now!"

Everyone froze at the sound of Tobias's bark. Bethan looked wide-eyed at Josif, who shrugged back. But Tobias was still glaring at Rolf, who shrugged the big man's hand off his shoulder. Still, he turned then toward the door as Tobias had indicated. While he might be seventeen and the tallest in the house now, Tobias still outweighed him by nearly double.

"Fine," Rolf snapped back. "But make it quick."

Tobias grunted, and Rolf followed him out the door, his neck hot and prickly.

Rolf couldn't say when it had started, but over the last

few months...or maybe it was over the last year, his protector had begun to change. He had always been opinionated and pushy, but Rolf had always understood that it was because he was trying to keep them all safe, and that wasn't an easy thing to do.

But something had changed. And though Rolf couldn't exactly say what, he knew innately that he didn't like it. From the look on Tobias's face now, Tobias knew it, too.

"You're seventeen now," Tobias began gruffly as soon as the door shut behind them, "so I'll get to the point." He looked up from the ground, directly into Rolf's eyes. "You need to send the girl back."

Rolf rolled his eyes. "Not this again."

"Rolf—"

Rolf fixed him with a wry smile. "You've been after me to exchange Bethan since she got here. I'm not sending her back just because she doesn't tickle your fancy. Good ganders, Tobias, she's been here eleven years!"

"That's not what I—"

"This is getting ridiculous." Rolf turned to go back into the cottage, but Tobias grabbed him by the shoulder and spun him around again.

"I'm being serious!" he hissed.

Rolf felt the heat in his neck triple as he shoved the meaty fingers off his sleeve. "Tobias—"

"That girl is no good for you!" Tobias roared, shoving him against the wall. "She never was, but even less so now! And you need to send her back!"

Rolf stared at him. Never, since they had left the old

world behind, had Tobias shouted like that. Rolf did his best to stand up straight under the large man's heavy hands, which he was now using to pin Rolf to the wall.

"And what brought this change on? New word about the faeries?" Rolf spat the last word out as though it were a curse. It was as good as to him. "You've hardly left the cottage to search for word of them in the last two months. You used to bring back all sorts of reports of them and of my father. And now you just sit around here stuffing your face and wasting time."

Tobias looked like he might burst a vessel in his temple. But then he took a few deep breaths, and when he spoke again, his voice, while no less intense, was quieter.

"I stopped searching so I could stay and watch *you*."

Rolf snorted. "Afraid I'll fall into a stream and get washed away?"

But Tobias didn't look away. "I've been watching both of you."

Rolf finally succeeded in standing up straight, and Tobias let him.

"Fine," Rolf said. "I'll bite. Why did you feel you had to suddenly nanny us?" He'd been more aware of Tobias's watchful gaze lately, but he'd thought it was simply because the man was bored and had nothing to do. He'd never suspected it was because Tobias thought he had to.

"You're seventeen," Tobias said slowly. "A man now, as I've told you."

"Which one would think would make me less in need of nannying, not more."

"Rolf," Tobias said with a huff. "You're a young man who spends his every waking moment trailing after a beautiful girl. Anyone who spent half a minute with you two could draw obvious conclusions as to what you want. And don't be naive enough to think Josif hasn't noticed. He's the one who told me how close you've gotten recently. Now, I may be old, but don't for a moment think I've forgotten what it feels like to want a woman with every bit of my being."

In spite of his anger, Rolf felt his face flush with a new kind of heat. "Josif and I have talked about this before," he muttered. Why did this make him feel so embarrassed? "He told me how to be respectful. And I have been. Besides," he raised his chin in defiance, "Bethan is as proper a lady as any."

"Be that as it may," Tobias said firmly, "you've been making every effort to sit closer to her than before. You touch her arm or her back every chance you get. And before you interrupt me, I'm aware that she won't kiss you. It's one of her few redeeming qualities. For a peasant, she's got class. Your mother probably would have approved of her without thought of her pedigree. She was known for that kind of thing."

Rolf bristled. "So what exactly are you warning me about now? If she's been the pinnacle of virtue, as she has, then why do you think she needs to be sent back into danger?"

"Because she's young and vulnerable," Tobias said in a strange voice. "And I'm not sure she'll be able to resist you much longer."

Rolf took a deep breath. If the outside world was as dangerous as Tobias liked to say it was, why in the blazes was he so sure being here would be worse? "Well," he said, straightening his shoulders, "that sort of worry won't be necessary after tonight."

"Oh? And why not?"

Rolf gave him a hard smile as he headed toward the door. "You'll see."

For a second time, Tobias's big hand grabbed Rolf's shoulder and yanked him back. But this time, his eyes were wild and fierce.

"You're not..." He searched Rolf's face and shook his head almost to himself. "No. No, I forbid it! You're not ready! You've not even seen the world. And being tied down–"

Rolf had had enough. This was getting ridiculous. "Tobias, I'm grateful for your concern. But I wish you were locked in your room until morning."

Immediately, the man disappeared. Rolf straightened his clothes then let himself back into the house, where he was greeted with shouting and banging from down the hall.

"Did you lock Tobias in his room?" Bethan asked, a wet plate still in her hand. Her eyes were wide, and she was staring down the hall.

"I did."

Josif, who had been sitting in the corner, whittling at a stick, looked nearly as shocked as Bethan.

"You don't need to worry," Rolf told the quieter brother. "Let me take my walk with Bethan, and you'll be fine."

Josif paled slightly and hunched further into his seat.

"Let me get my boots and cloak," Bethan said as she put the plate down. "I'll be right back."

Rolf nodded and began twiddling his thumbs. He was rehearsing his practiced lines in his head for the twelfth time that evening when Josif's thin voice broke the silence.

"You'll... you'll be good t'her... won't ya?"

Rolf blinked down at him. "Of course. Why wouldn't I?"

Josif's thin face turned bright red, and he nodded at the ground. "Thought so," he said in an even softer voice. "Just... her being'f age now and all..." He swallowed hard.

Rolf stared at him. What was wrong with the brothers? They'd all lived together for over eleven years now. And while Tobias had commanded Josif to teach Rolf manners and etiquette with ladies, which Josif had known a surprisingly bit about, they'd never made this much of a fuss about Rolf and Bethan spending an evening together. Rolf's first instinct was to tell Josif to mind his own business. But unlike Tobias, Josif was generally meek, and he seemed to genuinely like Bethan, so Rolf restrained himself. But Josif must really have felt some need to speak up if he had forced himself to do so.

But why?

"I'll take care of her," Rolf said, working to make his voice softer. "I always do."

Josif watched him for a moment before nodding as Bethan returned to the kitchen. Her curls were brushed and pinned back neatly again, and she was wearing the pretty blue and red cloak he'd given her for her birthday last year.

"Where are we walking tonight?" she asked with a smile.

Rolf smiled and offered her arm the way he'd seen in pictures in his books. She beamed and took it, and they set off together. Rolf's heart had never hammered so hard in his chest. And as he wished for the lightning bugs to accompany them into the twilight, he had no desire to look back.

CHAPTER
TWELVE

Rolf quietly wished the clouds away as they made their way to the edge of the clearing. Keeping them away was something he'd given up long ago, but he should have a good half an hour before they returned. More than enough time to enjoy the moon's silver light.

"Which one?" Bethan asked, coming to a stop. They stood between two paths, one leading to the north and the other to the west.

"Actually, I have a new path for us tonight," Rolf said, tugging gently on her arm. Bethan looked up at him in surprise, but he was pleased to see that she was smiling.

"Did you discover it, or is this a recent wish?" she asked as they began down a third path which led to the south. The incline began to rise almost immediately.

"The path is a wish," he said over his shoulder, leading the way so he could help her up the winding footpath. It hadn't seemed so steep when he'd completed the climb on his own a few days ago. "But the destination is one I found recently by accident."

"Did you mean to go this high?" she asked, sounding slightly out of breath.

"I did. I wanted to see what was up here." He paused and held his hand out. "Is it too hard? We can go another way if you like." As he spoke the words, his heart flopped into his stomach. He wouldn't force her to climb, of course. But all his plans...

"Do you doubt me?" She gave him a look.

He chuckled. "No. I know better than that."

"Right then. Lead the way."

Rolf did as she commanded, making his way up the path until they were both breathing hard. But just when he was about to ask if she needed to go back down or wanted him to wish them there, for he could see that she was favoring her right foot, they rounded a corner, and the land flattened briefly. A thick outcropping of rock rose above them like a sentinel, crystalline water pouring ceaselessly over its sharp edge. Below the waterfall was a little pond which was just as clear as the water that filled it, and from the pond flowed a stream. Little pink flowers lined the edges of the pond, and in spite of her exhaustion, Bethan let out a cry of delight when she saw the scene, and she ran to the pond and knelt at its edge.

"How did we never find this?" she breathed, staring into water which mirrored the moon and stars.

"We tried," Rolf admitted. "But I think we were too short the last time we attempted the climb. I only found this a few weeks ago when you sent me out looking for mushrooms."

"I know you won't appreciate the comparison," she said, giving him a wan smile, "but it's magical."

Rolf wasn't enamored with comparisons to magic the way his companions seemed inclined to be. But tonight, he had no qualms except with the subject of the comparison. The waterfall and pond, while pretty, were hardly worth such a word.

The girl, however, was another story. Her dark curls were edged in the moon's silver, and her pale skin seemed to be made of moonlight itself. Her lips were slightly parted as she studied the water, and her graceful form was angled forward like a statue in one of his books. The way she knelt at the water's edge now reminded him of their favorite childhood stories of nymphs and other fantastical creatures. She truly did seem like a fantasy, one that might dissipate into a wisp of smoke if he but blinked.

His stomach suddenly in his throat, he walked slowly to her side and sat beside her on one of the large rocks. He began to open his mouth to ask her the words he'd practiced endlessly for weeks. But the tear running down her cheek made him freeze.

"Bethan?" He gently turned her face to look at him, only to see that there wasn't just one tear running down her face. "Bethan, what's wrong?" He immediately knelt beside her.

She shook her head and looked out over the pond. "My family."

Of course, she was thinking about her family. He ought

not to be surprised. It was only natural. He'd spent a good deal of time thinking about his mother and father on his own birthday. But this direction of thought was hardly going to help him accomplish what he had planned. Still, he knew better than to push. So rather than fight the inevitable, he sat on the ground beside her and took her hand in his.

"How do you think your parents would have celebrated today?" he asked in a voice that sounded strangely unlike his.

She smiled into the dark. "I only know because my older sisters all had their seventeenth birthdays three years in a row." She laughed a little. "One—Efa—had a string of admirers a furlough long. Father nearly pulled his hair out with her. He gave his blessing to the first man who asked—I think just so he wouldn't have to worry about her anymore."

"Did she want to marry the suitor?" Rolf asked.

Bethan laughed. "She wanted to marry all the men who whispered about love and matrimony, so when one finally made the effort to ask, she was as pleased with him as she would have been with anyone else." She paused. "The twins were first, though. We didn't have enough money for all those fancy gifts you give me each year," she nudged Rolf's shoulder, "but Mother always found a way somehow to scrimp together enough ingredients to make a little cake for the one who was turning seventeen. My older brothers all got one, too, on their birthdays. Of course, whoever got the cake would share it with everyone else, which always meant the younger children ate more than anyone."

"What did the twins get on their birthday?" Rolf asked.

"Well, each got a dress. Really beautiful ones she embroidered for their wedding days, whenever those would be. And Father would make each a wooden trunk that he built all by himself, a trunk each girl could put her dress and other belongings in to take them with her to her own home whenever she got married. Then the whole village would come together and sing a song of blessing."

Bethan's eyes narrowed as they moved back to Rolf, and he knew instinctively what was coming next. "The faerie was a part of that, you know. She would deliver the final blessing to the man or woman coming of age, and usually, she would bestow on them a small charm of some sort, something that would bless them for the rest of their lives. One of the twins–Lowri–got a necklace that would keep her and anyone she was touching, warm and dry, even in the rain. The other twin–Krysta–received a blanket that would ease the pain of the person wrapped inside." Her voice caught as she spoke these last words, and they were silent for a long time.

Rolf looked down at the ground. "I'm sorry," he whispered.

She looked at him. "I know you are." Her gaze wasn't reproachful. But it was sad.

This was not going the way he had planned.

Rolf stared at the ground, hating himself as he never had before. He had never meant for it to happen this way. He hadn't asked for the wishing gift. He hadn't wanted the faeries to find him or to send him into hiding or to punish other children in his place. He had only ever wanted to keep his loved ones safe.

A soft hand touched his cheek. He looked up to see Bethan giving him a gentle smile.

"You said the book was my first present." She gave him a coy smile that sent his blood racing through his veins. "Where's my second?"

He had to swallow twice before he could answer. "I'm not sure you'll want it." He'd felt so ready an hour ago. But now...now he was sure he didn't deserve to give it.

She raised her chin and held out her hand. "Nonsense. Give me my present, Rolf."

He stared at her for a moment before a chuckle escaped him. "Very well." He stood, then he reached down and gently pulled her to her feet as well.

They were so close now. Her warm hands were clasped in his, and her slightly flushed face was so close he could feel her breath. Looking into her eyes was like gazing into the starry night sky, and her soft lips beckoned him silently. He forced his eyes back to hers.

"Bethan, before you came, I wanted to die."

All signs of mirth fled her face. "Rolf," she said softly. "You were six."

He nodded, suddenly unable to speak.

Slowly, carefully, she reached up and touched his cheek. Rolf closed his eyes, basking in the feel of her skin on his. "I had just watched my mother die," he said, eyes still closed. "My father and caretaker were endangered by my very existence. I was cut off from everyone who loved me, without a purpose or a reason for being. I felt like I had become a hole with no floor."

Tears were running down Bethan's face again, so he used his thumbs to wipe them away, a smile coming to his own face as he remembered.

"The first time I saw you, I knew I was looking at the most beautiful creature God had ever made." He paused. "I still am."

Bethan sniffed, and her cheeks reddened slightly more, but her eyes sparkled.

"I thought I was going to keep you safe. But you were the one who protected me. You taught me what it meant to be thoughtful and kind. How to reach beyond the wishes for a strength of my own. And while I'm...grateful for Tobias fulfilling my mother's wish to keep me safe, I'm far more indebted to you for helping me find life once again."

Rolf dropped to one knee the way the pictures in his books had shown, and with a shaking hand, he pulled a small object from his cloak.

Bethan, whose eyes were nearly the size of walnuts already, sucked in a fast breath as the moon caught the ring's shimmer and threw it around them.

The ring was made of silver with white gold filigree, but on it was a small pink flower no bigger than a bee. Its white diamond center seemed to have a glow of its own in the moonlight, and the pink gem petals surrounding it cast reflections as well.

"Marry me, Bethan," he whispered. "For even when we're free and can return to the world, there won't be anyone else I could or ever will adore more. You are life itself to me. And I never want to be without you again."

"You...you really mean it," she whispered.

He nodded. He had never been more sure of anything in his life.

Her eyes finally moved from the ring to his. And for a fleeting moment, he was sure he saw the glow of promise in them. But then she gave him a sad smile.

He suddenly had the urge to throw up.

"I love you, Rolf," she said, her voice shaking. "You are the sweetest, kindest boy I've ever known."

Wait? Boy? But he wasn't a boy. He was a—

"But I can't get married without my parents' blessing. And beyond that..." She sighed. "You don't know what you're asking."

Rolf frowned. "I'm asking you to share forever with me."

But Bethan shook her head. "Rolf, you think you understand the world."

"Bethan—"

"But reading about the world isn't the same as living."

Rolf stared at her. Was this really happening?

"You have no idea what the world is really like," she continued, turning and gesturing in the direction of the distant mountain valley to the north. "From what you've told me, you were sheltered from it before you even came here."

Rolf finally found his voice as he stood again. "That doesn't matter!"

"It does!" Bethan cried, pulling her hand from his. "And

when we do eventually leave this place, you're going to find that every foundation upon which your world is perched has crumbled."

"Whether or not that's true," Rolf said, shaking his head, "I *know* what love is. And I love you, Bethan! With all my heart. And that's never going to change!"

"But it could!" She pointed at the waterfall. "This? This is a faerie tale. You're afraid of the faeries, but you don't actually know what they are. You don't know what it means to tend to someone who's sick or work for a day's wages or shelter from a blizzard or even go to market! How can you know what love is?" Her tears had stopped, and her eyes sparked like fire.

Rolf's chest felt like it might crack in half. Pain and anger surged as he watched her take another step away. "You can't know that!"

"Then if you really love me, take me to the real world! Let me show you what that...that monster has hidden from you your entire life!"

"You know we can't do that! We might be seen. Someone could tell–"

"Then make us invisible!" she shouted. "But don't you dare tell me you love me more than life if you don't love me enough to grant this wish!"

They glared at one another, both breathing hard. As they did, however, Rolf's thoughts scrambled.

He didn't want to take them into the real world. If her beloved faerie saw them, everything might fall apart. According to a portrait of his father, Rolf knew he looked exactly like his father. It would be short work for a nearly all-powerful faerie to connect him to his father. Then what would happen to his father and their kingdom?

And yet...

He had said he loved her. And though he didn't want to admit it, a part of him, a part that had been growing louder as he grew older, wondered if she just might be right. Granting this request...it was risking everything. But he had meant it when he said he loved her and would love her forever. And if this was the only way to prove it...

So be it.

"Take my hand," he snapped. "And hold on tight."

She blinked at him as though surprised. He wondered if she had really meant it, but before he could rethink his offer, she put her hand in his.

"I wish," he said sharply, still holding her gaze, "that we were in Bethan's old village, invisible to both faerie and man." He had no idea whether or not the magic would hide him from faerie eyes. But he had been in his mountain retreat for eleven years without being seen. Surely he could make it through one short hour in the real world without being found out. At least, he prayed it would be so. Or he had just doomed his family and his kingdom.

The feel of cold smoke surrounded them both, and when he opened his eyes, he nearly dropped to his knees.

They were standing in the corner of a village square where hundreds of people roamed about. Women handed out small pies, and children chased one another with screams of delight. Men stood in clumps, holding tankards of mead and talking while the women laughed and shooed children away from the sweets. No one was dressed in anything finer than wool, and the cottages and stores that lined the square were equally humble, but no one milling about seemed to care.

"Oh!"

Rolf looked at Bethan to see her mouth open as she drank it all in.

"I'm home!" she whispered.

"Does everyone usually come out in the evening like this?" Rolf asked. The sun was setting, but men were lighting great torches erected in the ground, and several giant bonfires were lit in the center of the square.

"No, not usually. Tonight must be..." She counted quietly on her fingers before her eyes grew wide again. "It must be the Celebration of Lilies!"

"The what?" he echoed.

"Summer peak! We celebrate it by dedicating an entire day to the lilies that grow nearby! I'd forgotten that my birthday falls on the same week!" Then she let out a squeal. "That's my sister!" Still holding Rolf's hand, she dragged him through the crowd, expertly darting between people, horses, and carts. He let her lead him, suddenly feeling nearly overwhelmed by the size of the group. Had there been this many people at his sixth birthday? He couldn't remember.

"There she is!" Bethan pointed to a woman at least ten years older than herself.

Rolf studied the woman. She shared Bethan's blue eyes

and dark curls, and several small children with similar features danced around her feet. But there was something starkly different about her.

"Why is she so fat?" he called over the din of the square.

Bethan let out a peal of laughter. "She's not fat, Rolf. She's expecting!"

"Expecting what?"

"A baby!" Bethan stopped and turned to study him. "You really don't know where babies come from?"

He felt his face heat. "I...I know the basics. I just didn't know it looks like...that." Josif had, upon Tobias's command, taken him aside years ago and explained how children came into the world. At least, Rolf thought he had. But now Rolf wondered if Josif knew much more than he did.

A man came to stand beside Bethan's sister and wrapped his arm around her shoulder while placing his other hand on her very round belly. The action was strangely intimate, and for a brief moment, Rolf found himself imagining himself as that man and Bethan in her sister's place. The thought made him warm and slightly embarrassed all over. Partly because it was just so strange. But also...

Also because he realized he wanted it.

"Oh, that's my oldest brother over there!" Bethan cried, seemingly unaware of Rolf's internal warfare. She dragged him over to where a very tall man was carrying two buckets full of water for an older woman with graying hair. Bethan froze halfway to them, and her face went white.

Rolf looked back and forth between them before asking softly, "Is that your–"

"My mother," Bethan whispered.

A look he had never seen before crossed her face. And though Bethan had always been one to smile easily and had never hesitated to make her displeasure with something known, a sort of reckless emotion seemed to overtake her.

For the first time, Rolf realized that he had never truly known her. At least, not the way he thought he did. When he'd awakened that morning, he had been sure he knew everything about the girl he loved. Her favorite color was yellow, and her favorite flowers were the little pink ones that edged the pond he'd recently discovered. (He'd wished them there on purpose.) Her favorite food was honey, and she despised poetry but loved stories.

This look, though...

This look showed him a girl he was never supposed to know. The girl who had belonged to the family she gazed longingly after now. She should have been aunt to the little children running about their parents' ankles, and she should have been celebrating with the parents who smiled but had faces lined with pain. She should have been poor and in danger.

And happy.

"Look, Grandmother!" One of the children held up a flower for the woman with graying hair to see. Rolf was pulled from his musings when he realized the flower was letting off sparks.

"Oh!" the older woman cooed. "It's lovely!"

The little girl nodded. "The faerie gave it to me. She said it was to remember Bethan."

Rolf's blood ran cold, and he looked anxiously over at Bethan, half to make sure she was still there, despite having her hand in his. She was still there. But she was crying. And unlike her silent tears from earlier in the evening, she sobbed until her shoulders began to shake, and she had to pull her hand from his to wrap her arms around herself as though she were holding herself together.

"The faerie says today is her birthday," the little girl continued, seeming unaware of the tears in her grandmother's eyes as well. The older woman smiled through her obvious heartbreak.

"Yes," she said, her voice husky. "Today was her birthday as well."

Was.

They believed Bethan was dead.

The little girl pointed back behind her to a woman who was obviously a faerie. Not that Rolf had ever seen one. But the woman's radiant glow, her large spiderweb-like wings, and her bejeweled clothing made her race obvious. And to Rolf's horror, she walked right up to them.

Rolf's first reaction was to grab Bethan's hand and try to run. But Bethan refused to budge, and to Rolf's surprise, the faerie didn't so much as look at them. Maybe his wish to be unseen by faeries had come true after all.

"Melisa," the faerie said, her pale eyes warm as she greeted Bethan's mother.

Bethan's mother gave her a shaky smile. "Thank you for

remembering."

"I never forget," the faerie said gently. "Bethan is always in my thoughts."

"And you're... you're sure you haven't heard of her?" Bethan's mother asked, twisting her apron in her hands. "You don't know where she is?"

"Where she is, I cannot say," the faerie replied.

Could not, Rolf wondered? Or would not?

"But," the faerie continued, "I can tell you confidently that she is safe. I would know in my heart if my godchild were otherwise."

Faerie godmother.

Rolf's mouth dropped open.

Bethan had a faerie godmother. And she somehow knew that Bethan was safe.

Bethan's mother seemed to be expecting this. She heaved a long sigh before nodding with a sad smile. "As always, thank you."

Bethan, who had been frozen in place during the entire exchange, was no longer crying. Instead, she was smiling up at the woman peacefully. There was more trust in her face than Rolf had ever seen. She didn't even look at *him* like that.

After the faerie went away to greet someone else, Bethan wiped her eyes with her skirts. "Let's go find my father. I'll bet he's near the barn." Then she continued towing Rolf around behind her, telling him in a falsely cheerful voice about this person or that as they passed. But to Rolf, it was all a blur.

"Rolf?"

"What?" He looked up to see her studying him, her brows slightly furrowed.

"Are you well?" she asked. "You look sick."

He was sick. But what ailed him wasn't something that could be remedied with peppermint tea. Or even a wish.

"I'm well enough," he said, forcing a smile, though he doubted it looked any better than he felt. "Did you see everyone you wanted to?"

She studied him, her brows still slightly furrowed, before slowly nodding. "We can go back," she said slowly.

Rolf nodded in return and made the wish, his stomach swishing around inside him as he did. A moment later, they appeared in a darkened kitchen. Josif was asleep in a chair in the corner, and the hall no longer echoed with Tobias's yells.

"Are you sure you're well?" Bethan asked, real concern lining her face.

"I...um," he began before shaking his head. "I just wanted to let you know that I might be a bit late waking up tomorrow. I...I have some thinking to do. Make whatever breakfast you want and do whatever you need."

Alarm sharpened her gaze. "Rolf, about tonight, I—"

"No." He tried to smile. And failed. "You were right. We're not... I'm not ready."

"Rolf—"

"Good night, Bethan." He leaned down and kissed her forehead. "And happy birthday."

Then, without looking back, he went to his room.

THIRTEEN

Lying on his bed, not bothering to take off his clothes, Rolf stared at the ceiling.

Since witnessing his mother's death, Rolf had believed all Tobias had ever told him about the world and faeries and...and everything. After all, he'd seen his own mother murdered. And the constant stream of news of the faeries' mischief had kept him on his guard all the years after. Each time Bethan had convinced him to consider visiting the real world, Tobias had regaled him with all the ways doing such might harm him. Or worse, her.

Only his desire to prove his love to Bethan had been enough to change his mind. His desperation to prove to her that he truly was in love and that he wanted her forever was able to do what fear hadn't and break down the walls of fear he'd built around them.

He'd expected, of course, to see a piece of Bethan's

world. Knowing what he did, however, of the wiles of the faeries, he'd also expected to see darkness that she didn't.

But Bethan had been right.

He wasn't ready.

Not because he didn't love her the way he had professed. He would love Bethan until the day he died. She was everything meaningful in his life. But now that he understood just how little he knew of the world, and how ill-prepared he was to be who she needed him to be, he was forced to draw a bitter conclusion.

His love wasn't enough. Nor would it be any time soon.

"I wish..." he said slowly, the wish taking shape in his mind as it had been doing since he got home, "I wish..."

This wish would need to be thought out carefully. Whatever this wish did to him, he knew instinctively that its repercussions would be lifelong. What he wished for tonight would affect not only his fate, but Bethan's, as well as his father's and Auntie Alicia's and every soul in what should have been his kingdom.

What he wished tonight would change everything. It would either confirm everything Tobias had been saying for years...or it would upend Rolf's entire world. For once, though, Tobias wouldn't be around to answer his questions, and neither would Bethan. This time, the question would be answered by stark, uncensored truth.

Though, if he was honest with himself, after witnessing Bethan's old village with his own eyes, Rolf had a feeling he knew the answer already.

"I wish," he said more clearly this time, "to see what happened to my mother."

He smelled the familiar white smoke around him. And once again, he was standing in a little room.

He'd never been anywhere like this, but he guessed few places, homes or shops or whatever this was, were as filthy as this one. The floor looked as though it had been covered with wooden slats at one time, but so much dirt covered it that Rolf couldn't be sure. There was a little bed beneath a pile of moth-eaten blankets in the corner, and a messy pile of firewood plastered with cobwebs in the corner. A dark wooden trunk stood in the corner by the fireplace, and a hunched figure sat on a stool by the fire, mumbling to himself as he puffed away at his pipe.

The door opened, and a tall, familiar figure stepped inside before closing the door firmly behind him. He was breathing hard, as if he'd been running.

"What do you want?" the figure on the stool grunted. Though his words were rough, the voice itself was oddly silky smooth.

"I'm told you sell charms," a younger Tobias gasped.

Rolf frowned. What did Tobias have to do with any of this?

"I don't talk to men in hats. Uncover yourself or leave."

Tobias glanced at the window, which was too covered in grime to see through, and removed his hat.

"My price is high," the huddled figure continued. "Higher still if you need something unusual. What kind of charm are you looking for?"

"A sleeping charm," Tobias huffed. "One that works right away. Oh, and one that imitates a dead body, but so torn it's unidentifiable. And I need them *immediately*."

The huddled man grunted again. Then he went over to the big wooden chest and began to rummage about in it. Several times, he held up a particular trinket, but only on the fourth did he seem to find what he was looking for. He nodded once to himself, then slunk back to his stool.

Rolf did his best to study the object he held in his hands. It was a small clay mug, the kind a child might drink from. "Want it to disappear after you cast the charm?" the old man asked.

Tobias nodded. "I can't afford to leave a trail."

"It'll cost you extra."

"I can pay it," Tobias said, looking very much as though he wasn't sure he could.

Still, the old man nodded again. "Good." Then he took out a gnarled stick and began to wave it over the clay mug. Only then did Rolf realize the stick was really a wand.

Silvery magic floated from the wand to the mug, the old man muttering the whole time. This went on for several minutes. Tobias continuously glanced back at the door.

"When you want it to work, you'll smash it on the ground just beside the person you wish to put to sleep. Don't breathe any of it in, or it will put you to sleep, too." He went back and rummaged through the trunk again.

"For the body, leave this," he held up what looked like a bone where the mug had been, "on the ground wherever you want it. Everyone else will see what you want them to see." For some reason, this made the faerie grin, revealing for the first time, the lower portion of his face.

Such a beautiful face. And such a dark smile.

The faerie named the price, one which made Tobias pale. Still, he pulled the amount out of the little money bag that hung from his belt. Then he snatched up the bone that had been a mug, and tore out of the dirty hovel so fast the door slammed behind him.

Then Rolf was transported to a foreign place once again.

Only...it wasn't foreign at all. His breathing hitched, and his knees threatened to buckle as he looked around the menagerie. It was evening, just before dusk, and his father's castle rose up into the darkening sky like a mountain. Now that he was taller, Rolf could see over the fence to the large hedge that surrounded the cottage he had shared with his mother and Alicia. And coming through the gate before him was *her*.

A sob caught in Rolf's throat as he saw her, young and perfect, bedecked with jewels and covered in beautiful satins and silks. Dark circles sat beneath her eyes, but a familiar smile was on her lips as she led a guard carrying a small dark-haired boy through the gate.

She didn't see Rolf standing before her, his mouth open as he drank in the sight of her. He thought he'd remembered her well, but even his magic portraits didn't do her justice. Every mannerism was as familiar as his own, and tired as she seemed to be, her voice was gentle and low as she pointed to a little rise in the grass by the pond.

"This is the perfect place for him to rest. And after I

awaken him, he shall walk to the cottage." She hesitated. "He was near far too many people today. I wish for him to remain healthy. Fresh air will help clear out his lungs."

Healthy? Why wouldn't he be healthy? Rolf didn't remember ever being sick as a child. And if he had gotten sick, all he would have had to do was wish it away.

The guard seemed confused by her wish to put him on the ground by the pond, but he obeyed quickly. Auntie Alicia, who hadn't been far behind, told his mother that she was going to fetch some tea.

Only when Rolf was clearly snoring on the ground did the queen allow her true exhaustion show. She leaned back against a tree not far from where Rolf was lying and let out a deep sigh. There was a pain in her face Rolf didn't recall, although now that he considered it, he supposed it couldn't be easy raising a child who could wish into existence everything he wanted.

How strange that this day so long ago had been the hinge on which his entire life had turned.

Rolf was still musing to himself when a familiar prick in the air caught his attention. He knew the sensation of magic well, and he cried out for his mother to pay heed. She couldn't hear him, though. Of course, she couldn't. This, after all, was only a memory.

Rolf quickly located the source of the magic. It was the clay mug being held over her head by someone in the tree.

That someone was Tobias.

Tobias was hanging in the branches above her. He didn't

linger there, however. After dropping the charm, which closed the queen's eyes and made her flop over onto the ground, the big man jumped down and used some animal's little house to climb up and leap over the fence, his landing surprisingly quiet on the other side.

Young Rolf had awakened by now and was begging his mother to open her eyes. Rolf's entire body felt racked with pain as he relived the darkest part of his life, far worse than any nightmare.

Tobias leaped back over the fence as though he hadn't just been in the tree, and snatched up the young boy and began to carry on about how he had to get him to safety, how the faeries would be back to steal the young prince away. Rolf felt his own young wails echo through his memories. He pressed his fist against his mouth as his deeper wails mingled with the boy's.

But when he opened his eyes again, he was back in his room on the mountain. His face was soaked, as was his pillow, and he could hear Bethan's voice coming through the door.

"Rolf? Rolf, what's wrong? Let me in so I can see you. Rolf!" Her voice was anxious, and the lock on the door rattled.

But Rolf didn't want to let her in. He didn't want to face her, knowing that what he had been told...everything he had done to her...had been based on a lie. So instead, he made a new wish.

"I wish," he said, his voice breaking as he spoke over her

now panicked cries, "to know everything that happened to my family. And everything that was hidden from me." He paused as the white smoke began to encircle him.

"I wish to learn everything I should have known."

CHAPTER
FOURTEEN

Rolf ought to wake up.

He had known this for a long time. More than once since he made the wish, consciousness had begun to steal through him. But each time he was nearly ready to return to the world, some other scene would appear in his thoughts, and he would dive right back into the unknown, engorging his mind with something new he might have missed.

It was easier that way. Learning meant not considering the repercussions of all that the lessons meant.

A scraping sound came from the corner of the room, and though he wished to escape once again, Rolf sighed. It was time. He couldn't escape the world any longer. No matter how much he wanted to.

When he tried to open his eyes, however, they seemed... stuck. Rolf had to rub them several times to get all of the crust off his eyelids. After several failed attempts, they finally fluttered open. Only for him to slam them shut again.

The light coming from his right seemed all wrong. It was intensely bright, far brighter than the light from his window had ever been. And the rest of the room, including the side that should have had another window, was completely dark.

The air was also far colder than it had ever been.

"Rolf?"

Though he had been loath to open them for his own purposes, Rolf's eyes flew open at the sound of Bethan's voice. It had come from somewhere near the bright light. Steps hurried to his side, going so quickly that she tripped over herself and half-fell to the ground beside him.

"You're awake!" she cried, taking his face in her hands. Then she looked him up and down before grasping her hands in his and holding them tightly.

A moment passed before he was able to see clearly, so sensitive were his eyes to the light, but after several hard blinks, Rolf stared.

Bethan's face, which had been round and alive with color the last time he'd seen her, was pinched and thin. Small lines sat at the corners of her eyes, and her clothes were worn and patched in many places.

"What..." He struggled to prop himself up on his elbows, which was harder than it should have been, as his arms and shoulders were impossibly stiff, and looked around.

They were no longer in his room, which would explain the strange brightness to his right. Instead, they were in a cave. The blinding light came from its mouth, and over the cave's mouth poured crystalline water.

They were in a cave.

Rolf pushed himself into a sitting position and looked around further. He had been placed on a pile of blankets on the ground. Another pile of blankets had been made up in the far corner of the cave, and a small fire pit had been dug in the center. They were sleeping on the floor, similar to the way his mother had let him...

His mother.

"Bethan!" he croaked, looking up at her in wonder and awe. "My mother! She's alive!" He sounded more like a frog than a man, but he didn't really care. Tobias had lied about many things. But he couldn't be more overjoyed that his mother's death was one of them.

"Rolf, that's wonderful!" She smiled at him, but her smile was a ghost of the one he remembered.

"What..." he began again, licking his dry, cracked lips. "What happened?"

She blinked at him several times. "Rolf, you've been sleeping for two years."

He stared at her. "Two *years*?"

She nodded, glancing nervously at the cave's entrance. "The night of my birthday...after we returned from my village. You said that you would most likely be sleeping in late the next morning and not to wait for you. So I didn't. But then midday came. And afternoon. Then night. Then the next day. And the next, and..." She swallowed. "You just didn't wake up."

Rolf rubbed his head.

Two years.

"I...I never meant to sleep for..." He scrunched his eyes shut and tried to get his head to stop spinning.

"Eventually, Tobias told Josif it was time. He'd played at this game far longer than was safe." She drew in a shaking breath. "He ordered me to kill you."

Rolf gaped. "He did...what?"

"He said he'd purchased some faerie trinkets in his time away, and if I would kill you, he would send me home. He said he'd found my old village, and that he would send me there and leave me alone forever if I did as he said."

Rolf felt his stomach harden into a lump of stone. "But you stayed. For me."

"I could never *kill* you," she whispered, the corners of her eyes glistening. "You know that."

Unable to speak, Rolf simply squeezed her hands.

"When I wouldn't kill you, he decided he was going to do it himself. But Josif...Josif didn't want to kill you either. So he helped me bring you here. And then he told Tobias he did the job, and that he had killed me too."

"Where are they now?" Rolf asked, anger beginning to simmer beneath the shock.

"They've gone. Although, Tobias keeps his riches here. I don't think he can move them anywhere else. He still uses that charm you gave him to travel to and from. So I have to take care when I go out to forage for food or take from the garden that he doesn't see me." She took a deep breath and let it out slowly. "Rolf, what happened? Why did you sleep for two *years*?" Her words were slow and painful, and Rolf hated himself for it.

"I..." It felt so strange to speak, like his tongue was a foreign object and not a part of his mouth. "After we returned home that night, I decided that I needed to know."

"Know what?" she asked.

"Everything."

She studied him for a moment before her eyes widened. "So for the last two years—"

"I've been learning. I've seen everything that was hidden from me. As a child. As a man. What I ought to have learned from my father. What I should have known as a boy." His throat constricted. So much more than that, even. The truth about disease. Poverty. War. Disaster. The rise and fall of nations. Loss. Anguish. Grief. Pain.

So much pain.

His throat tightened until it ached. "The truth about my mother's death."

She sighed. "It was Tobias," she said softly. "Wasn't it?"

He nodded then mashed his hands against his eyes so they couldn't leak.

Bethan, as always, however, seemed to understand, standing and seating herself on his blankets beside him. He put an arm around her and leaned his head on hers as she huddled, small and shaking, against his shoulder.

They stayed that way for a long time. Bethan's body seemed to drain of strength as she leaned against him. Rolf did his best simply to keep breathing as the weight of all he had found crashed in on him, threatening to crush him. The loss of his innocence was heavy.

"What are we going to do?" Bethan finally broke the silence as the sun began to set. Her voice sounded so brittle, as if it might shatter into a thousand pieces.

Rolf had thought he loved her two years ago when he had sought her hand in marriage. And he had in his own way. But he had been a boy then. Now he was a man. And as a man, he knew that he loved her a thousand times more than he ever had before.

He also knew he needed to let her go.

"I'm going to—"

The sound of crunching gravel from outside the cave made them both freeze.

"... don't know why we're 'ere," grumbled a thin voice. It was Josif's. Rolf was sure of it.

"Because the charm I left behind was awakened this morning," came Tobias's gruff reply. "Which is interesting, considering you told me you killed them both."

Rolf stood slowly, doing his best not to make a sound. He motioned for Bethan to stay on the bed where she sat, his mind working fast.

Tobias was a villain, but he was no fool. He hadn't, it seemed, fallen for Josif's trick, and it seemed he'd left a faerie charm for himself so he would know whether Rolf was alive.

That they had to leave was obvious. But where should they go?

The voices grew closer.

"...able to buy charms that should track his magic. If he uses any once off this mountain, the charms should tell me exactly where he is," Tobias continued. "And I've got even worse things in store for her." He snorted. "And if I find out that you helped her, so help me..."

If Rolf wished them back to Bethan's village, Tobias would find them. He had made it clear in his threat to Bethan that he knew not only where she lived, but that he would hunt her down if she disobeyed him. If Rolf took or sent her home, that would be the first place Tobias would look. Rolf could, of course, wish a number of evils upon the man, but who knew what other hidden charms Tobias had already put in place to prevent such a thing? After all, as a naive boy, Rolf had wished up a fortune for the man to use as he pleased. For all Rolf knew, Tobias could have a number of faeries at his own beck and call thanks to all his gold.

No, for the time being, until he figured everything out, Rolf would need to remain hidden. And even more so, Bethan would as well.

Rolf put his hand in his cloak, and to his surprise, he found the small flowered ring still there.

The footsteps grew closer.

"I wish," he whispered, "that Bethan was safely hidden in this ring."

"What?" Bethan turned to look at him.

"In the cave!" Tobias shouted. "I heard something."

I'm sorry, Rolf mouthed as the white smoke began to encircle her. Just as Bethan disappeared, a hulking frame filled the cave entrance.

Tobias, though a good deal rounder than he had been two years before, looked somehow stronger as well. Rolf slipped the ring onto his smallest finger as Tobias took a step toward him.

"Where is she?" he snarled. "I need you both dead." At these words, he turned and glared at his brother.

"It's just me," Rolf said, holding his arms out. "And I wish you were unconscious."

He glared triumphantly at the man. But the white smoke never came. Instead, Tobias just grinned.

"You think I didn't expect something like this eventually?" He clucked his tongue. "It's going to take some special wishing to get at me, boy. You gave me a vast sum of money. And thanks to a few faeries of my own, I've collected a vast sum of protection charms myself." He smirked. "As well as several curses waiting for the girl as soon as they find her."

"I wish your protection charms were broken!" Rolf shouted, taking a step backward. But he nearly fell backward when his ankle hit his blankets. "I wish you would fall from a cliff!"

Tobias only snickered again.

"You can keep trying if you wish." He removed a knife from his vest. "I'm enjoying myself. It proves to me that I am a wee bit clever after all to outcharm you. Keep the wishes coming."

Rolf tried to think fast. Obviously, whatever charms

Tobias had purchased were more potent than the magic Rolf had been gifted with. He couldn't stop them. But maybe...

"I wish your traveling coin was broken!" Rolf cried.

Tobias froze. "You..." Then his skin reddened, and he charged Rolf.

Josif, who had been glancing back and forth between Tobias and Rolf, was faster. He leaped at Tobias from behind. But Tobias whirled around and stabbed the knife into his shoulder.

"No!" Rolf shouted as Josif made a choking sound and stumbled backward. "I wish Josif was healed and that he and I were in a field in the countryside alone!"

This time, the white smoke began to fill the cave. Tobias's eyes grew round. Raising the knife over his head, he sprang at Rolf.

FIFTEEN

The magic whisked Josif and Rolf away just as the dagger tore through the front of Rolf's shirt. Then it dumped them in a large corn field.

A wheezing sound made Rolf look down. Remembering that he wasn't alone, Rolf fell to his knees.

"No!" Josif shook his head, his face contorted with pain as he gripped his left shoulder with his right hand. "No magic! His charms..." His words became a groan.

Rolf's stomach lurched at the blood soaking through Josif's shirt. But even as he gaped, the wound, visible through the shirt's large gash, began to close over.

"It's all right," Rolf said, nearly laughing with relief. "The wish worked. It's healing!"

"Much 'bliged to you," Josif groaned as he sat up.

"It appears we're obliged to you," Rolf said, taking the flowered ring off. "Bethan would never have been able to get me into that cave without your help." He lifted the ring.

"No!" Josif cried, grabbing for the ring. "'Member, no magic!"

Rolf yanked his hand back, cradling the ring against his chest. "I can't leave her in a ring!"

"Can't bring 'er back!" Josif shook his head vehemently. "M'brother wasn't lyin'. Bought a load'a curses and sent 'em chasin' after 'er. Thought she'd a'been found already."

Rolf stared at him, his stomach roiling again. "But I only–"

"Tobias blames 'er for everythin'," Josif said sadly, still staring at the ring. "Made you ask questions'n thinkin' 'n and all."

"I just want to send her back to her faerie godmother in her village," Rolf said.

But Josif shook his head again. "'At's the first place he's got 'em curses. Th'float around just lookin' for 'er. He's got 'em all over!"

Rolf studied the thin man. This complicated things. If he couldn't send Bethan home, and Josif seemed convinced she wasn't safe anywhere, what could he do with her? He couldn't keep her in a ring forever. He'd only meant to keep her there for a few minutes so he could get away from the brothers before they could find her.

The brothers.

Then a new kind of alarm hit him. "Speaking of questions, why are you helping us?"

"Beg yer pardon?"

"I said, why are you helping us?" Rolf took a step back.

"After all these years, when you could have told me the truth, you've only decided on honesty just now?"

Josif stared at him, a deep red coloring his sunken cheeks. Then he looked at the ground. "Tobias'n me always went together. I was never much for head knowledge n'all that. M'parents said I was dumb as'n ox. But Tobias kep' watch for me. Kep' me fed'n housed when m'parents said they'd not feed me no more." He shrugged. "When we first got y'from the castle, he said we was makin' you free, away from yer mum's rules and all that. But the longer we was there..." He sighed. "I knew t'wasn't right. The lyin'. The stories. Makin' up bad proof and all that. But who...what was I to stand up to m'brother?" Josif paused and peeked shyly up at Rolf.

"You did stand up, though," Rolf said cautiously. "Why now?"

Josif shrugged again and traced the toe of his boot in the dirt. "Didn't want to do murder."

Rolf swallowed and studied the man for another long moment. Yes, Josif had lied to him for his whole life. But of the two brothers, Josif had always been the kindest by far. And now, he had saved lives.

"Very well," Rolf said slowly. He turned and surveyed their surroundings. There wasn't a road in sight. Mountains edged the western horizon, but the majestic peaks were so far away that they were little more than shadows in the evening light. There was, however, a farmhouse visible in the distance. And as Rolf had no idea where they were, it seemed the best place to start. "Let's go then."

Josif's head snapped up. "What...you mean go with you?"

"Why not?" Rolf asked.

"Y'mean you're—"

Rolf gave him a ghost of a smile. "You did save my life. Twice. I'd say that's reason enough to take anyone along."

Josif looked for a moment as if he might cry. Then he fell into step behind Rolf and followed as Rolf began toward the farmhouse.

As he walked, his mind spun.

He needed to get to his father. And he needed to talk to a faerie. He briefly considered wishing himself to Bethan's old village to find her faerie as fast as he could, but as it seemed Tobias had left all sorts of curses there to find Bethan, that plan seemed risky, even if she was trapped in a ring.

Of course, going home wasn't going to be an easy feat either.

For one, his mother was still alive. This thought alone kept his feet moving, one in front of the other, rather than allowing him to give into despair. His mind had been too addled from sleep when he'd first awakened to really understand the consequences of what had happened, but now he was fully aware of all he had to do. And if anything could motivate him to go home, it was the knowledge that his mother was alive.

Unfortunately, she had been imprisoned since his disappearance, locked in a tower for the last thirteen years. Tobias had seen to that, along with help from a few ambitious courtiers. And while she had been sentenced leniently compared to what the court had desired, the king still believed her responsible for allowing Rolf to be taken. The rest of the court, of course, thought Rolf was dead.

Still, his best chance at finding a faerie was to go to his father's court, for in all he had learned about the world during the last two years, he'd discovered that his father was one of the wealthiest, most powerful kings in the realm, and if a faerie was likely to visit anyone upon request, it was a rich and powerful king.

But he would have to take care with how he dealt with his father. The man, while always proud, had become distant and suspicious since what he believed to be his wife's betrayal. Getting close to him would be difficult.

He could, of course, wish everything to rights. But—aside from the dangers Tobias had created when it came to using his magic—if Bethan had taught Rolf anything over the years, it was that wishing had limits. And while one might force the human mind into some sort of submission, as he had done once or twice to Tobias when Tobias had thrown a fit over the food Bethan had cooked, the conviction was lacking.

Rolf's mother deserved justice.

Bethan deserved justice.

But neither would get it until the entire truth was revealed and the hearts of his family and his courtiers were fully convinced of the veracity of Rolf's claims. He had seen for himself what had happened. Now he had to prove it to the rest.

Silently, Rolf determined to himself that he hoped to

never use magic again if he could help it. Magic had taken nearly everything from him...and from those he loved. If it hadn't been for his mother and Auntie Alicia, and then for Bethan, magic would have turned him into a monster. No, he would only use magic in the gravest of circumstances from here on out.

But without magic, how was he supposed to get close to his father?

Now that he had seen his father in his dreams, Rolf knew he was a near perfect reflection of the king. Appearing at the palace wearing the king's image thirteen years after disappearing would throw everyone into a panic. No, he would need a way to get into the court and the king's confidence on his own merit, something that would bring down the king's guard. He would need to offer something the king enjoyed. Which, after watching the events of the past thirteen years unfold, seemed like very little.

Rolf stopped and turned around. "You lived in the palace with your brother while Tobias worked in the kitchens, didn't you?"

Josif frowned for a moment then nodded.

"Tell me, do you remember anything my father was passionate about? Something he loved dearly?"

Josif scrunched up his face. Then he beamed. "The queen!"

Well, that was touching. But not helpful.

"What about...something he liked to do?"

"I don't..." Josif let his thought trail off. Then he sighed. "Can't recall. Sorry."

Rolf tried to give him an encouraging smile, though he felt anything but encouraged. "Just think about it, I suppose. And let me know if you remember."

He could, of course, wish to know. But the wish might reveal something the king didn't share with his courtiers. It could also, of course, alert Tobias to their location. No, the best way to find out what the king loved would be by finding something that even people like Josif would know.

They walked for another hour before they reached the farmhouse. The couple there agreed to let Rolf and Josif sleep in the barn if they would help with the chores in the morning. The woman who lived there also insisted that they eat with the couple as well, for both of them, according to her, needed fattening up.

Rolf and Josif were just about to go to sleep when Josif let out a cry. Rolf, who had been teetering at the edge of unconsciousness, bolted upright.

"What is it?"

"Huntin'!" Josif said proudly. "The king likes huntin'! After you gave'm all that money an' he bought 'mself an earlship, Tobias even went with'm one time!" He paused. "With the king, I mean."

This time, Rolf's smile was real. "Excellent work, Josif."

Josif grinned and nodded once to himself before lying down. Rolf lay down, too, but he wasn't sleepy anymore. No, now that he knew the way to his father's heart, all he needed to do was plan.

CHAPTER
SIXTEEN

Rolf was determined to refrain from all magic as they made their way to the palace. But even his determination was tested by the fourth day, when he was sure he might never walk without a limp in his right leg again. He'd never walked so much in his life, and after two years of sleep, with every step he took, his body was reminding him of that now.

The only upside to all the walking was that it gave him more time to plan.

The more he thought about it, the more he was convinced he couldn't simply walk up to the castle and announce his survival. He had learned enough during his two years of sleep to know that humans didn't like surprises. Especially not when they'd spent thirteen years thinking someone was dead. His father had grown suspicious since Rolf's disappearance and his wife's sentencing, and anyone who claimed to be his long-lost heir was more likely to end up in the dungeons than the throne. In fact, during his two years' sleep, he'd seen it happen more than once.

Of course, there was also the problem of his resemblance to his father. His facial hair had begun to grow out, but it was growing so slowly he wasn't sure it was even worth the effort. He'd only ever tried to grow a beard once, back when he was fifteen. He'd spent hours trying to trim that beard to perfection, and while Bethan had blushed slightly and thought it looked nice, Tobias had laughed so hard that Rolf had wished it off that night before going to bed. Still, this one should be much easier. He was going to pose as a hunter. And no hunter needed a perfectly trimmed beard.

But that was only his first problem. His second problem was his mother.

Rolf was still reeling from the knowledge that his mother was alive. Not only was she alive, but according to his dreams, she'd been charged with neglect of the crown prince and shut up in a tower as punishment. A number of courtiers had wanted her hanged, something that brought Rolf close to revoking his decision to avoid magic. If it hadn't been for the fact that he worried his magic would draw the attention of Tobias and his purchased faerie charms, he might have. But he didn't know how many magical alarms Tobias had set out to find him and Bethan, and he didn't want to risk finding out.

He also knew deep in his heart that the justice meted out by the law would be better than the revenge he wanted to partake in.

No, he would do this himself. He would find his mother and save her. He would expose the traitors to his father. Then he would find a real faerie and convince him or her to break the curses that were somehow searching for Bethan and bring her back to humanity safely.

Things would be set to rights, even if it killed him.

ROLF WAS BEGINNING to agree with Josif, who claimed they would never reach the castle, when—on the seventh day—they arrived at the capital.

Rolf would have been surprised at the size of the city surrounding the castle, except for the many visions he'd had of it in his sleep, when he'd learned about the history of his fathers. They stopped at the edge and stared over the thousands of rooftops at the castle spires that glinted in the sun over the city.

"I'm afraid I can't have you come with me to the court," Rolf said, looking apologetically at Josif. "You were with Tobias for years. I'm sure they'll know you."

Josif waved him off. "I know places t'go."

"I'll search for you when I'm done,"

Josif gave him a sad smile. "Prolly best if y'didn't." Then he looked out over the rooftops again. "But I knows my way here. It's all right now." And with that, he took his walking stick, which he'd found in a nearby wood, and made his way down a side path into the city. Rolf watched him go for a full minute before starting down the main road, which he assumed led to the castle.

The walk was long, and though Rolf had been taught the ways of the world in his dreams, he was constantly surprised by the variety of smells found in the streets and stalls of the city. They were potent and putrid, as well as floral and sweet. Baskets were filled to the brim with plump fruits, vegetables, roots, and grains. Pigs squealed and doves cooed from their respective cages as he walked by, and several times, children ran into the road as though horses and carriages didn't exist.

Mercifully, Bethan had had the sense to strap a small bag of gold to his belt. She must have assumed they'd want to travel fast. He never would have had the insight for such a thing. Giving a silent prayer of thanks, he stopped briefly to purchase a bow and some arrows from one stall, and an apple from another, then he continued on his way. It was nearly two hours later when, dusty and rumpled, he stopped before the king's gate.

The gate, nearly twice as tall as a house and just as broad as one, was open. Finely dressed people rode in and out on horses and in carriages while those in more common clothes walked or pulled carts. Rolf pulled the hood of his cloak over his head and looked down as he walked through. The guards seemed to be rather relaxed, but it would be best not to waltz in showing everyone the king's face on his own.

Josif had informed him that the line to petition the king was open every afternoon for several hours. Unfortunately, the line was always very long, and less than half the people were seen every day. Rolf had insisted they wake early that morning so he could arrive at the castle and get in line early, but he was disappointed to find that even in the late morning, two hours before the king would begin to hear complaints, the line of hopefuls already snaked out of the castle and into a courtyard. Somewhat dispirited, he took his place at the back of the line and waited.

Still, as frustrated as he was to have to wait to speak to his father, knowing his mother was inside the building that towered above him right now, there was a strange sort of... enchantment—he could think of no other word for the sensation—at being...

Home.

Because he was home.

He remembered this place. It was like awakening from a dream and then choosing to step back into it. A nice dream, the kind that one never wanted to leave. He'd only been here at the castle once that he remembered, but the sounds were like a song from the past, and the smells of the surrounding trees and grasses were frighteningly familiar. His mother's cottage hadn't been in this area, he knew, but it must have been close by, close enough for him to instinctively know the sights and smells of this world.

Likewise, when he finally made it into the castle, he was assaulted by another wave of familiarity. Which was odd, as he'd only spent his sixth birthday here. And yet, that day was imprinted upon his memory like a seal upon rich wax.

Awestruck as he was, however, he soon became anxious again. The line was moving ever so slowly, and he knew by the tolling of the bells that the king would leave his audience soon. Ten more minutes, and he could see the archway that led into the throne room. Five minutes, and he was four places from the front. Finally, he was able to see into the throne room.

And there was his father. It truly was like looking into a mirror. Rolf had to remind himself to breathe.

"His Royal Majesty will return tomorrow to hear more requests from his people!" a herald called out.

Rolf's heart stopped as his father rose from his throne and made his way toward a side door.

This couldn't happen.

"Your Majesty!" he shouted.

The entire room, including his father, looked at him. Two guards took a step in his direction.

"I'm a hunter!" he continued to shout. The guards were at his side in a flash, but he kept going. "I've heard you collect unique trophies, and I come bearing gifts!"

At this, the king turned to fully face him. The guards took Rolf by the arms and began dragging him backward, but Rolf stared doggedly at the king, unwilling to break eye-contact. He needed his father to hear him.

Because if he didn't, this was going to be much harder from the dungeon.

"Wait!" the king called.

The room went silent.

"Bring him here."

Rolf sent up a prayer of thanks as the guards put him on his feet and began escorting him to the king.

Then suddenly, Rolf was ten feet from his father, and his knees suddenly had the urge to buckle.

"Who are you?" the king asked, folding his hands.

Rolf willed his knees to work and bowed low. "I am Rithindir, master hunter of the wilds, faerie–blessed and eager to prove my worth to His Majesty."

"A faerie–blessed hunter?" the king repeated, raising one brow. "I will admit that this intrigues me."

"I wander often," Rolf said, glad he'd practiced his lines so many times on the road. "So when I heard that the great King Albert was a hunter at heart, I made my way here to see if I could impress such an impressive sovereign."

"Did you?" His father chuckled. "Well, you have heard correctly." He took a step closer. "Have you...um..." His smile faded, and he squinted slightly. "You look familiar."

"My father was born at this castle," Rolf said with a smile of his own. "There is a good chance you see his face in mine." Hopefully, the king didn't see *too* much.

To his relief, the king smiled again. "Another happy connection. Well, hunter, I can only assume that you have something you desire in return for your gifts." He frowned at Rolf's empty hands. "Wherever they are."

Rolf opened his mouth but hesitated. He had to take care. Ask too much, and he would raise suspicion. Ask too little, and he might as well have gotten a room at an inn.

"I wish to dine with the king," he said. "And, if it is not above my station, perhaps I could spend a night or two in your servants' quarters while I prepare my gift."

"And what is this gift that needs preparing?" the king asked.

Rolf took in a deep breath. "That, Sire, depends entirely on you. What do you wish me to hunt?"

This was the trickiest part of the entire scheme. He had thought long and hard about how to earn his father's trust. Whatever it was, he hoped it would earn him deep enough trust to allow him within the walls of the castle so he might seek out his mother. He just hoped the king didn't have his sights set too high.

His father's eyes brightened. "You are *that* confident are you?" he asked softly.

Rolf smiled. "I am my father's son."

The king broke into a grin. "Well then, Rithindir, I will gladly feed and house you...once you bring me the head of the Ghostly Stag."

Rolf's heart fell.

"I've heard it told," the king continued thoughtfully, "that the head of such an animal would bring good luck to the land in which it dwells. It's said to run about the forest north of here, but for the life of me, I haven't been able to find it." His eyes narrowed slightly. "You think you could find such a creature?"

Rolf did not. But he worked to keep the smile on his face. "Of course, Your Majesty." And with that, he bowed low again and made his way to the door. As he left, however, he wanted to curse.

The Ghostly Stag, of all prey.

His father might as well have asked him to bring him the head of the Queen of all Faerie.

Rolf had read about the Ghostly Stag in a number of the story books his wishes had kept him supplied with. While it truly was a stag, and not a faerie, as some faeries preferred to keep the forms of creatures, it was sacred to all faeries. Ages before, legend had it, a faerie had found the creature as a fawn, starving and ready to die. She was young herself, and though lacking the magic to heal him at once, she'd hand-fed the creature back to health. It had been her cherished pet after that, and as she grew, so did her power. She had gifted the creature an ageless life, and over the centuries, other faeries had come to love it as well. Its presence was considered a good omen for the kingdom in which it was spotted.

Rolf had no desire to kill the faerie-favored creature, nor was he stupid enough to wish to try. He was already stuck with magic he didn't want. The last thing he needed was to have some awful curse added to the blessing he was trying to get rid of as it was. But he hadn't been able to think of anything else to say to his father that would keep him within the castle walls.

Rolf walked down to the harbor and sat down at the edge of a dock, where he took Bethan's ring off his finger. "What am I supposed to do?" he murmured to the ring, turning it in his hands. How he longed to wish her out of the ring and back with him. She would know what to do. But just as he was afraid to use such miniscule magic as to help grow his beard, he knew better than to use the magic to return her. He wasn't close enough to reaching his goal.

"Just a little longer," he sighed before putting the ring safely back on his smallest finger. Then he stood and ate his apple as he stood and made his way toward the forest.

What he would do when he got there, he hadn't the faintest idea. But all he could do was go.

SEVENTEEN

When Rolf reached the forest, it was nearly night, and he was glad he'd already purchased the bow and arrows. Though many skills were beyond his reach, he was actually decently skilled with the bow. The year he'd turned twelve, Bethan had informed him that while he may be safe in his forest, it would behoove him to learn some self-defense.

"My brothers all learned by the time they were ten," she had said with a sharp nod. "And it would be best if you knew how as well."

"Where am I supposed to learn?" Rolf had asked. "You keep telling me not to learn things with magic."

Bethan's blue eyes twinkled. "I'll teach you."

As it had turned out, Bethan's oldest brothers, much to the horror of her mother, had decided it would be a great joke to teach their baby sister how to hunt. And so Bethan had spent months teaching him until she had declared that he was as good as she.

Now he held his bow tightly as he made his way quietly through the brush. The Ghostly Stag wouldn't harm him. At least, not as long as it didn't know what he was doing. But other creatures might.

He walked for several hours until he was near the heart of the wood where the stag was most often spotted. Then he stopped at a tree with low, thick branches, and climbed up to wait.

He waited for three nights.

Knowing he wouldn't see the stag during the daytime, he would climb down and buy himself something to eat. Unfortunately, his little bag of gold began to run low on the third day, so Rolf bought himself a few extra pieces of fruit and a loaf of bread with the intention of staying within the wood until he had spotted the deer.

As he sat, he continued to turn the matter of what to do with the stag over in his mind. He didn't want to kill the deer. He didn't need to eat it, and it had done him no harm. But there was no other way to get and stay within the walls of the castle.

There was no other way to free his mother and Bethan.

The faeries would punish him for sure once they discovered what he'd done. His father might have been ignorant about the importance of the deer, but Rolf wasn't. Still, if he did summon an angry faerie by killing their majestic creature, surely the faerie would listen to him before cursing him. He didn't care if they cursed him further. But the faerie would surely listen to his pleas to help his mother and beloved.

Or perhaps, not so certainly.

The crack of a stick awoke Rolf from the fretful doze he'd fallen into, and when he turned his head to see what had caused it, he nearly fell out of the tree.

A stag nearly two heads taller than Rolf had stepped out of the shadows to graze on berries from a bush. But it wasn't the size of the majestic stag that had Rolf frozen on his branch. It was the way it glowed.

The stag had a faint blue glow that emanated from its hide, though where the light came from directly, Rolf couldn't tell. Its hide was white, which, cast in the faint blue light, looked exceptionally similar to the way Rolf imagined a ghost would appear. Its eyes were a piercing blue, and its antlers looked as though they were made of marble. After Bethan, it was the most beautiful creature Rolf had ever seen. Especially when it turned and met his gaze.

They stared, eyes locked, for what felt like eternity.

But then Rolf was reminded of what he had come to do, and his spirit fell.

His hands were already clasped around the bow, as they had been for days, and the arrow was already loosely nocked. He raised the bow slightly for his mother. And then a little more for Bethan. But just when he had nearly aimed it perfectly...

He groaned and doubled over, rubbing his temple with

one hand, the arrow falling from his grasp into the bushes below.

He couldn't do it. He couldn't destroy this beautiful life so his father could have another trophy.

"I wish there was another way," he whispered. And then he realized just what he had done. And if he'd been frightened before, it was nothing compared to the horror he felt now.

He hadn't meant to make the wish. He'd been so lost in his agony, torn over how to do the right thing, that he'd simply said the first words that came to mind.

The familiar smoke began to swirl on the ground below, and Rolf froze in his spot. He expected the stag to run, but instead, the stag approached whatever was appearing. Then it bent its head, and a hand with several sparkling rings reached out of the smoke cloud and rubbed its head.

Rolf thought he might pass out. It was a faerie. And not just any faerie. It was Bethan's faerie.

"Come down from the tree, Rolf," she said, sounding slightly amused as she continued to pet the stag. "Four days is long enough to sit in a tree, don't you think?"

Rolf scrambled off his branch so fast he nearly fell out of the tree.

"You...you knew I was there," he said after bowing deeply. "And...I suppose you knew what I was doing."

"I know what you didn't do." She quirked a beautiful brow at him.

Rolf felt shame heat his face. "I nearly did."

She finally turned away from the deer and faced him.

"It's true. And I would have been most angry with you. But I know why you're here." Her voice softened. "And the fact that you refused to do something evil even to accomplish something good makes me think all the better of you for it."

Rolf dared to look up from the ground. "Will you help me?"

She smiled sadly. "I cannot fix it for you, if that's what you mean."

He blinked at her. "But why?"

She drew in a deep breath and tapped her cheek with her finger for a long moment. "When I gave you your gift, I knew what it would lead to. In fact, that's why I gave it to you."

Rolf couldn't believe what he was hearing. "You...I don't understand. You gave me this gift? But you're–"

"Bethan's faerie godmother? Yes, I am that, too." She laughed, a sound not unlike Bethan's, only richer and deeper. "Do you think I would allow my goddaughter to be abducted by just anyone?"

More shame heated Rolf's face. At this rate, he might just as well melt into a puddle.

"I never meant to take her," he said quietly. "I really believed I was helping her."

"No six-year-old boy in his right mind would mean to take another child," the faerie said softly. "You were acting on the lies upon which you had been fed."

Rolf took several deep breaths, trying to fight down the sudden rush of emotions that were warring within him. "But I don't..." He squared his shoulders and looked straight at her. "Why would you let all of this happen? To my mother? To Bethan? To me? None of it would have—"

"If I had let you grow up in your father's court, you would have become just as blind and short-sighted as he and his ancestors have been for generations."

"But I've hurt so many people," Rolf whispered, his voice suddenly shaking.

"You would have hurt many more if you had grown up the way you were supposed to." The faerie flicked one of her wings. "We all hurt people. It's the nature of sin that stains us all. Humans in particular, but we faeries have our share as well. Rather than remaining in your ignorance, however, as your father would have encouraged you to do, you have changed."

Rolf frowned. "How do you know that?"

The faerie smiled. "You didn't loose the arrow."

"But—" He stopped.

She was right.

"And not only that, but you sought to learn what you did not know. You have made plans to follow the law by righting what has been made wrong. And while I might not have chosen your exact...path to accomplish such," the faerie smiled, "I believe you are on your way to completing the journey that you must in order to be the person your people need you to be."

Rolf took the ring off his finger and held it out. "Would you take her at least? Let her out and give her back to her family?"

The faerie looked sadly at the ring. "I'm afraid I can't. Not yet, anyway."

"Why not?" Rolf demanded.

"Because your intuition about Tobias's magic was quite accurate. He went to a faerie that practices dark magic and bought charms which he then unleashed upon the world. If I could *find* the charms, I could dispel them quickly. But as they travel, I can't stop them until I know where they are."

Rolf wanted to throw up. "You mean... she's stuck like this?"

"I never said that. What I did infer, however, is that *you* will have to stop Tobias to free those he's entrapped in his web."

Rolf shook his head. "But if you can't stop him, how can I—"

"It's not that I *can't* stop him." The faerie snorted. "I could make him drop dead on the spot if I wished."

"I don't see the problem with that," Rolf muttered. "He deserves it."

"You are right. He does. But then how would justice be served? Who would testify to your mother's innocence?" She arched one perfect brow.

Rolf heaved a sigh and sat on the ground, rubbing his face with the heels of his hands. "That's easier said than done. I have nothing to take back to my father. Which means I'm back to the beginning."

"Not necessarily." The faerie smiled back at the stag, who was nibbling at the berries again. As soon as she looked at him, he raised his head and approached her.

"Your father isn't as terrible as some of his actions might make him seem, nor is he nearly as awful as that mother of his. And I'm convinced that a gift of similar magnitude will please him just as much as an offering like that for which he asked." She held out her hand, and the stag lowered his head. Carefully, the faerie plucked the antlers off the stag's head. Then she handed them to Rolf, who was so surprised that it was a moment before he realized she wanted him to take them. Though they were separated from the ghostly deer, they continued to glow blue in his hands.

"But won't he—" Rolf began, but the faerie interrupted him.

"He sheds them every year," she said, rubbing the stag's head gently. "And he would much prefer to give you these than his life."

Rolf was once again glad that he'd read so many books on lore as a child. Years of those stories weighed heavy enough in his mind to remind him to stand and bow to the deer.

"I thank you," he said solemnly. The stag stared at him for a long moment before nuzzling Rolf's shoulder once and then returning to the berries.

"Your journey isn't over yet," the faerie said, taking Rolf by the arm and drawing him closer. "You must find a way to convince your father of the truth. And after thirteen years of believing one way, changing his mind will not be an easy thing to do."

Rolf looked down at the antlers. Surely...surely this would be a good start. It had to be.

"And not only that," the faerie continued. "You were also correct in guessing that accessing your magic with a wish would draw Tobias's attention. He purchased a number of charms that would alert him should a wish be made and left them all over the countryside, anywhere he thought you would be. He's back in the capital city now, which means that Bethan, your mother, and even you are in mortal danger. I will do my best to seek out the curse charms he's placed about, but I cannot guarantee I will find them fast enough. You'll need to hurry back and make sure you're in the king's good graces before Tobias worms his way back into court. And," she added thoughtfully, "you'll probably want to abstain from using more magic if possible. I can only guess that his charms will call even more attention the more you use it."

Rolf swallowed hard. "Thank you."

The faerie seemed to read his thoughts because she drew him into a motherly embrace. The sensation was strange, almost like reaching back in time to when his mother did the same.

"Don't hate your father," the faerie said quietly as she let him go. "He's a product of his upbringing, just as you are." Her eyes bored into Rolf's. "None of us would bear the scrutiny of the world, should we be put on its stage. Only...take this opportunity for what it is and learn what he did not."

"It would be easier if everything were black and white," Rolf grumbled.

"If only it were." The faerie laughed and shook her head. "Now, I cannot stop what has been begun, but with this blessing, I'll speed you on your way to its conclusion." She leaned forward and kissed Rolf's forehead. Then the world began to turn as it filled with smoke, a sensation Rolf knew only too well.

When it stopped turning, he was on the castle steps. And the morn was about to dawn.

EIGHTEEN

Rolf might have been bothered by the dirty looks the castle attendants continued to throw him as he waited on the castle steps, but he was too tired to care. His exhaustion was so complete, in fact, that when he saw the king crossing a nearby courtyard with several well-dressed men, he had the audacity to scramble to his feet and call out to him.

"Sire!"

The king paused and began to look around, but a guard hurried toward Rolf, bearing a spear.

"You!" the guard shouted indignantly. "How did you get in?" He grabbed Rolf's sleeve and tugged hard. "You'll have to wait—"

"Hold, Quintus," the king called, striding toward them. The guard looked scandalized, but the king's eyes lit up the moment they rested on the horns. "That isn't a buck's head," said the king. His face, however, broke into a wide smile. "But I'm willing to guess there's a story where these came from." He leaned forward and ran his finger over the antlers reverently. "You can feel the magic humming through them," he murmured, almost to himself.

"He snuck onto the palace grounds before the gates were open, Your Majesty," the guard grumbled.

"He was on an errand for me," the kind said, straightening. "I would have been disappointed if he had made me wait." He turned to Rolf. "Come break fast with me. I haven't heard a good hunting story in ages."

Rolf bowed and did his best to act as any honored hunter would, despite the nearly deafening voice in his head that screamed for him to search for his mother now. No, he would have to earn that right. Hopefully, it would be his before long.

The king led him back into the castle and down a series of corridors until they reached a hall that boasted the longest table Rolf had ever seen, a roaring fire, and about a dozen courtiers already seated. Everyone stood when the king entered the room until the king went to the head of the table and was seated in a large chair. He indicated the bench on his right.

"Sit here," he told Rolf. "And tell me about how you came to possess these antlers."

Rolf bowed again before seating himself. It was so strange, he reflected as a plate heaped with food was placed before him. For so many years, he and Bethan had played castle using whatever information they could find in books or squeeze out of Tobias. He had thought that he knew everything there was to know about court etiquette. But now, he simply hoped it was enough. It wouldn't do to annoy the sovereign and get tossed out, even if the sovereign happened to be his father.

"I waited for three nights in a tree deep in the forest," Rolf began, aware that the man to his right was glaring at him, presumably for taking his seat at the king's right hand. "But when the fourth night came, I finally spotted the stag."

"I presume you didn't hit him with one of your famed arrows," the king said, eyeing Rolf's quiver.

"I did not." Rolf dared to look directly into his father's face. He watched him carefully as he spoke. "When the moment came, I found that I could not."

"You could not?" the king's eyes widened. "An interesting sentiment for a hunter."

"I was raised to hunt for food and other needs," Rolf said, slightly defensively. "Not for death itself."

The king sat back and studied Rolf. Rolf wasn't sure if this was a good sign, but he held the man's gaze, unable to keep all of his resentment away. It was this man's fault, and the fault of his fathers, that Rolf, his mother, and Bethan had been subjected to so much pain. He had sentenced Rolf's mother–his own wife–to solitary life in a tower for the negligence of their son. He was the reason–

Don't hate your father. The faerie's words came back to him.

Rolf wanted to hate him. He desperately wanted someone to blame. But his own guilt flooded his heart as he fingered the ring on his hand.

179

"You look...familiar," the king said slowly.

"I told you," Rolf said, looking back down at his food. "My father worked here."

But the king only frowned more deeply. "I don't think it's that," he said, rubbing his chin. Then he shook his head and picked up a bread roll. "So continue your story, how did you get these antlers if you wouldn't loose the arrow into this deer?"

So Rolf related the story of the faerie coming to the aid of her pet, and how the stag offered his horns in place of his life. He omitted, of course, the part of the discussion that surrounded his blessing and Tobias. He expected his father to sneer and scoff, but instead, the king only watched him thoughtfully. When the story was finished, he remained quiet for several minutes.

"So you were blessed for showing mercy," he finally said.

Rolf nodded once.

"Interesting," the king said. "Quite interesting. Yes, I believe this story was well worth my time. As are these." He lifted the antlers, which were leaning against Rolf's chair. He ran his fingers reverently over them in turn. "I'll have to request a faerie's assistance, though, in knowing what to do with them."

As late as yesterday, Rolf would have jumped for joy. A faerie had been just what he was looking for. But now he...

What was he supposed to do? He supposed he could use magic now. But no, the faerie had said to abstain. So what could he do?

"You said you wished to sup with the king and spend a

few nights under my roof." The corner of the king's mouth turned up. "Was that all you really wished for?"

This was it. The faerie had been right.

"Not entirely," Rolf said carefully. "I wish...I had one more request, if it's not too audacious for the king."

"On the contrary. You have me quite intrigued. That a faerie-blessed hunter would risk being cursed by the faeries at large in order to be welcomed into to my court has me most curious." The king rubbed his mustache. "Please tell me."

Rolf took a deep breath. "I wish...I want to seek justice."

"Oh?" The king frowned slightly. "Have you been wronged?"

"Yes, but it is not my suffering I wish to right. It's that of my mother and...and my beloved."

"Justice for your ladies. Even nobler. Please go on."

"When I was small, just a boy," Rolf said, watching his father carefully, "a man saw that I was faerie-blessed. And he stole me away from my family in order to use my gifts."

The king's face darkened to an alarming shade. "Did he?" he said in a deep voice.

The king's reaction was so strong that for a moment, Rolf's anger warred with satisfaction. His father hadn't forgotten him. Now, if he could only redirect that anger in the right direction...

"Then he blamed another for my loss," Rolf continued carefully. "And now that I am a man, just when I thought I was to be free of him, he returned. And he threatens to harm the woman I love by means of dark magic if I do not do as he says."

The king stared into the fire for a long time without speaking. But just as he opened his mouth, the doors opened, and the king's attention was drawn to them.

"Tobias," he said, his voice still rumbling like thunder, "come in."

CHAPTER
NINETEEN

Rolf froze. He instinctively wanted to look up at the man who had tried to kill him more than once, but he forced himself to look at his plate and took an oversized bite so he couldn't speak. Perhaps, if he laid low, he could escape Tobias's attention. Tobias had never seen Rolf with a beard, after all.

"Your Majesty," Tobias called, bowing low. Unlike the last time Rolf had seen him, he was bedecked in a ridiculous number of silks, gold chains, and silver rings with precious jewels. Rolf could hear a smile in his captor's voice and had to restrain himself from running the man through with an arrow on the spot. Doing so would accomplish little more than using magic, in that it would do nothing for the queen's reputation or the charms that stalked Bethan. No. Rolf would do better to wait.

"Sit and eat, Tobias," the king said, waving a hand at the

large man. "I'm not done listening to this young man's story." He turned his attention back to Rolf. "Go on."

"I wish to bring this man to court," Rolf continued, working to keep his voice even, "so that he may clear the name of those he perjured and be aptly punished for his crimes."

"You were taken as a boy, you say," the king said, with a thoughtful frown. "How old were you?"

Rolf swallowed. He could feel Tobias's eyes on him now. He must not allow his voice to shake. "Six years, Your Majesty."

"Taken?" Tobias called from the other side of the table. "Who was taken?"

A rush of rebellion took hold of Rolf, and against his better judgment, he allowed himself to look directly into his captor's eyes. "I was."

Tobias stared at him for a long moment. Then he turned pale.

"What's wrong with you?" the king sneered at Tobias. "And what do you want? Why are you here at my table?"

Josif had said that Tobias had worked his way into the king's favor at one point. Rolf could only guess it had to do with the mass of wealth Rolf had given him as a child, back when Tobias had said they needed it for safekeeping. But now, judging by the king's tone, Rolf wondered if Tobias had worked his way out of favor as well.

"I...I only came to pay my respects," Tobias said with a forced smile. "And with a contribution of my appreciation, of course."

So it *had* been Rolf's gifted wealth that had put Tobias in the king's good graces to begin with.

"Oh," the king said. "Well, I shall speak with you after I finish with Rithindir." He turned back to Rolf. "We shall speak more of this later. I greatly desire to hear it." He swallowed hard and glared down at his plate. "If it were possible to get such justice for my own son, I would have it at any cost." He shook his head and took a deep breath, suddenly looking as though he were ten years older. "You asked for a room, if I am correct?"

Rolf bowed his head. "If it pleases the king."

The king nodded. "You shall stay until justice is meted." His dark eyes burned. "You have my word."

Rolf had the strangest desire—one he had not felt in a very long time—to embrace his father. It was a strange sensation because he was still angry. The faerie had cursed him with this gift because of his father and their line. His father had also been the one to lock his mother in a tower, for a crime she never committed. And yet...

Rolf had told the faerie how much he wanted a black and white world, one in which every motivation was clear and understood. But the faerie had said such a thing was impossible. Not even a day later, Rolf was beginning to see that for himself.

Tobias looked as though he was ready to fall off his bench as Rolf stood. "I am most indebted to you for your gracious reception of a poor hunter," Rolf said, bowing deeply once again. "I do hope that I might have the king's permission to sleep for a few hours now, as I have been awake for many nights, searching for the stag."

"Of course." The king nodded. Then he gestured to one of the servants who was standing nearby. "Get this young man a room and a change of clothes appropriate for supper with me tonight, as well as anything else he might require."

Rolf bowed again and thanked the king once more before meeting Tobias's gaze as he followed the servant out of the hall.

ROLF'S ROOM was in another wing up several flights of steps. He wondered how long it would take Tobias to find out where he slept. Not that he intended to sleep now. He had work to do. And his first order of business was to ask a very impertinent question.

"Where, if I might ask, does the queen reside?" he asked the servant, who was throwing open the room's curtains.

The servant, a man who appeared to be slightly older than himself, looked scandalized. "The *queen*?"

"Yes," Rolf said with his best grin. "I wish not to disturb her should I get lost."

"Sir," said the servant curtly, "the queen has been locked in a tower since she was found guilty of negligence when the young prince was killed over a decade years ago."

"Ah," said Rolf. "My apologies. I haven't been to this

realm in a very long time. Pray tell, where is the tower so I might avoid it then?"

The servant still looked annoyed. "Stay where you're invited, and you won't have to worry, will you?" And then he was gone.

Rolf let out a curse as the door closed in his face. How was he supposed to find her now? Wander the castle?

Well, he would if he could. And if he was caught, he would feign ignorance. (Though, in all honesty, ignorance wouldn't really have to be feigned.) He could simply tell whoever caught him that he was lost. He waited until the man's footsteps had faded from the hall, and was about to step out again when a voice sounded behind him.

"That was well-maneuvered, though you could have done without directly challenging Tobias to his face."

Rolf, who had nearly jumped out of his skin, turned to find the faerie standing by the window.

"You...you're..." He tried to catch his breath.

"I'm here, yes. And I've been quite interested in your progress. You've made a good deal of it in just a few hours. But you have little time now that Tobias is here, and I wish not to see him get away again."

"Do you know where my mother is?" he asked.

"Of course, I know. But will that really help your case against Tobias?"

Rolf scoffed. "I haven't seen her in thirteen years. Don't you think—"

"I can tell you where your mother is," the faerie said, her voice gentler this time. "But you do have *very* little time.

Tobias's charm maker, I have discovered, is in this city. I have no doubt he will be running off to get more charms as soon as he has the king's leave. And these ones will be aimed at you."

Rolf hated that she was right.

"Can't you stop the other faerie?"

"If I wanted to start a war within Faerie, yes. But as it so happens, waiting for my queen is far wiser. Besides, when I've been busy locating Tobias's other charms. It's harder than it sounds." She folded her hands over her voluminous skirts. "So, where will you begin?"

"I don't even know," Rolf scoffed. "I need proof that Tobias framed my mother and abducted me. But the only ones present to see were my mother and myself. And my mother was unconscious for nearly all of it."

"But there was someone else," the faerie said patiently.

Rolf stared at her for a moment before understanding dawned. "Do you...do you think I should wish for him to testify against himself?"

"Considering the nature of the magic involved, no, I wouldn't recommend it."

Rolf huffed. "I'm not sure what I'm supposed to do then."

The faerie gave him an annoyingly patient smile. "You'll think of it. In the meantime," her voice softened, "visit your mother. She's in the tallest tower. I'll make sure no one finds you along the way."

DESPITE HIS ANNOYANCE with the faerie, Rolf was thankful for the safe passage as he followed her directions to his mother's tower. It was indeed the tallest tower in the castle, and Rolf was breathing hard by the time he reached the top.

The door to her chambers was made of thick wood, but if he listened closely, Rolf was able to hear two women's voices inside.

"Please take some tea, Your Highness. You haven't eaten anything all day."

He knew that voice, frustration whispered inside of him. But whose voice was it?

"Thank you, Alicia," said another voice. "But I'm not hungry."

If hearing the first voice had been a shock, hearing his mother's voice was like being dropped from a turret. In his mind, a thousand tiny moments, moments he thought he'd forgotten, seemed to come alive. Cuddles and kisses and hugs and laughter and scolding and lullabies. Rolf began to shake. He shook so hard he had to clench his teeth together so he didn't bite his tongue as he trembled.

Someone inside began to walk, but it wasn't until their footsteps stopped on the other side of the door that Rolf realized that he had no place to hide. As the key clicked inside the lock, he dove behind the tapestry that hung outside the door. He thought he was safe after the door was locked again from the other side, but before he could breathe easily, the tapestry was yanked back. And Rolf found himself face-to-face with his mother's best friend.

They stared blankly at one another for a long moment. Her eyes and mouth had more lines than he remembered, and she was a little stouter. But the shape of her face was as familiar to him as his own.

As he was reflecting on this, however, Alicia's face twisted into one of ferocity that he'd never seen as a boy, and for a moment, he was afraid she would scream.

"Who are you?" she hissed instead. "And what are you doing near the queen's chambers?"

Rolf tried to speak, but his voice seemed lost.

"Answer me," she hissed again. This time, however, she unsheathed a dagger from an unseen place on her hip.

"Auntie Alicia!" he whispered, putting his hands up. "It's me! Rolf!"

"You can't—" she began, but then she squinted at his face. And she dropped the knife. It clattered to the floor as she threw her hand over her mouth and shook her head. "But..." she said, her voice muffled by her hand. "It can't—"

"Shh!" Rolf whispered again. Then they both froze as his mother called out.

"Alicia? Are you well?"

"Um," Alicia scrambled to grab and resheathe her dagger. "Yes. I just...dropped something. That's all." Then she turned back to Rolf. "How did you...What...?" She seemed incapable of finishing a thought. Rolf understood the sentiment.

"I'm here to free her," he whispered. "But I have to find

proof first." He took her hands eagerly. "Did you see what happened?"

"Oh, love," she breathed, touching his face gingerly. "No. No, I'm afraid I had gone to get your mother tea. I only returned after you were gone."

Rolf sighed. "Nevermind. I'll find something." His gaze hardened as he looked at his mother's door again. "I will."

"I...I have to go, or they'll realize I'm missing," Alicia said, wringing her hands as she glanced down at the spiral stairs. "What can I do?"

"For now? Nothing. I'll send for you if I know of anything."

She nodded, seeming as though she was searching for words but couldn't find them. Finally, she took two steps toward the stairs, but he caught her by the wrist once more.

"Whatever you do, don't speak to Tobias."

Her eyes went wide. "Tobias? The one who used to be the castle cook?"

"That one." Rolf felt his fury flame. "He's not safe."

She gave him one more long look before squeezing his hand. "Be careful, love." Then she smiled sadly. "You might be a man now, but to me, you'll always be that sweet little boy to me. I wish I could do more, but..." She glanced anxiously down the spiraling stairs once again.

"Go," he said, though he wished very much to keep her with himself. Having an ally would make him feel far better. "I'll be fine."

She nodded but continued to frown as she made her way down the stairs.

Once she was gone, Rolf turned back to his mother's door. She didn't sound strong. If he weren't so afraid of being discovered, he would have asked Alicia to tell him how she was. But her voice had been so weak, and suddenly, Rolf knew instinctively that he shouldn't let her see him. Not yet. She wasn't ready.

But he could speak with her.

"Nadine," he called softly through the door. "How are you?" It felt so strange to speak her name, but he had the feeling that calling her Mother might be too much.

"Hello?" his mother called out. "Who's there?" Her voice was brittle and hollow.

"I was sent," he said slowly, "to see to your well-being."

There was no answer for a long time. Just when he was about to ask again, she called out softly,

"Are you an angel?"

Whatever Rolf had been expecting, it hadn't been that.

"No, I've... I've come to seek your justice."

"You are an angel," she said, her voice almost a sigh. "I've been waiting for you for a long time." Then, in slightly stronger tones, she asked, "Do you know about my son, angel? Does he still live?"

Rolf closed his eyes and willed his voice to be strong.

"He's... he's well, Your Highness." His voice broke twice. "He misses you dearly."

Another sound came from the other side of the door.

"Your Highness?" he called out.

"I'm only praying, angel. I'm praying because I am content. And the Lord may take me now if it pleases Him."

194

"What–"

"My son is alive," she continued through what sounded like tears. "That's all I've ever wanted to know. And now I feel complete."

Rolf only made it halfway down the countless steps before his vision was too blurry to continue. So he let himself collapse onto a step and leaned into the cold, hard stones as he felt himself break.

Being broken was nothing new to Rolf. He'd never felt completely whole since the day Tobias had taken him and told him that his mother was dead. There had always been a gaping hole inside of him, one he tried to fill with Bethan and carving and books and everything in-between. But everything he had ever tried to fill that hole with had been cleared away. The wound was just as raw as it had ever been.

And the wound was also far from clean. His own actions made it fester as his guilt crashed down on him anew.

Taking out the ring, he turned it carefully in his hands.

"I'm sorry," he whispered, trembling again. "For every-thing. For taking you away from your happy home. For keeping you all those years. I thought..." He was shaking so hard now he could barely speak. "I'll make it right. I prom-ise. You'll be free, and you'll have everything you deserve. And I'll never hurt you again."

ROLF HAD no idea how long he sat on that step. But eventually, when the light began to fade, he stood and slowly made his way down to the main part of the castle. Lost in his own thoughts, he rounded a corner without looking where he was going.

And ran smack into Tobias.

Tobias was the one to overcome his shock first. "You!" He grabbed Rolf by the collar and slammed him into the wall so hard that Rolf's vision was briefly filled with spots. "I knew you'd come back, but I didn't think you had the gall to come here. I–" He stopped and looked down to where Rolf had drawn his own dagger and was now pointing it at Tobias's large belly.

A woman screamed from Rolf's left. He and Tobias both jumped when they saw that three young ladies were staring at them, open-mouthed.

"Pardon, misses," Tobias said, letting go of Rolf's shoulders and slapping him on the back. Slapping him hard. "Young lad surprised me, that's all."

The women didn't look mollified in the slightest, and Rolf used their surprise to put his dagger away. So rather than inspire gossip, Rolf bowed low. "My ladies. Forgive us for acting as brutes. We hadn't realized such beauty was at hand."

Bethan would have rolled her eyes up into her head if she could have heard that. She despised flattering speeches. The girls, however, looked amused.

"Might you," he asked, flashing what he hoped was a charming smile, "point me in the direction of the king?"

His smile must have been convincing enough because the shortest of the group giggled and held out her arm. He took it, and in a moment, was being escorted away by all three girls while Tobias remained fuming behind him.

Whatever Rolf was going to do, he needed to do it fast.

CHAPTER
TWENTY

Though Rolf did find him, the king was unavailable to meet with him for the remainder of the afternoon and early evening. Still, he was again given a place of honor at the king's side for supper, which was a lively affair.

At least, it seemed lively enough for everyone else.

The king spoke little. He responded well enough to anyone who addressed him, and he would often ask probing questions of those around him, but Rolf didn't miss the way his eyes darted from face to face to the door and back again, as if expecting an interruption at any time. Rolf was reminded of his two years' education when the magic taught him what he had missed. He had seen enough to know that his father trusted few.

The king also ate little, despite the rebukes of his mother, whom Rolf was introduced to over supper.

"You're getting hideously skinny," the queen mother

hissed when she thought no one was listening. "No one can look up to a king who might be blown away by the next wind."

Rolf wouldn't call his father skinny by any means, but it was true that since he had seen him in visions of the past, his father was far thinner than he had once been. In fact, he was nearly the girth he had been when Rolf was small. But the deep lines on his face and the dullness of his eyes when no one was watching told Rolf something that disarmed him far more than the faerie's words.

His father was a good actor to the untrained eye.

And he was deeply unhappy.

Rolf wasn't allowed to focus solely on his father or his plans for that night, however. Tobias continued to glare at him over the table for the length of the entire meal. And Rolf was sure that if he didn't find a way to prove Tobias's guilt quickly, he would never get the chance. Then Bethan would remain trapped in the ring, and his mother would die alone in her tower.

Supper came and passed, however, with no revelation. In desperation, when the king began to rise, Rolf took a gamble once more.

"Sire."

The king looked at him with such an expression of weariness that he nearly faltered. But the feel of the ring on his finger forced him to continue.

"Sire, I was hoping I might have a word with you. Alone." Rolf's heart pounded in his chest as the king's brows rose in surprise. It was an audacious thing to ask of a sovereign, particularly when one had known him less than a week.

"You need your rest," the queen mother said in a low, sharp voice as she shot an accusing gaze at Rolf. But Rolf refused to meet her eyes. Instead, he focused on his father, who studied him silently.

"Very well," the king finally said. "Come with me to my study and we'll talk."

"Albert," the queen mother hissed. "What is this boy to you?"

"I don't know," the king said, looking over his shoulder at Rolf once more. "But...I have the strangest feeling I need to find out."

Rolf followed the king and his personal guards to the king's chambers. They were on the same side of the castle as the queen's tower and more lavishly decorated with rich reds and golds than Rolf had ever imagined a room could be. Not even Tobias could have imagined this kind of luxury.

I should be familiar with this place, Rolf thought to himself as he sat in the chair indicated by the king. And that made him sad. What would it have been like to run and jump on the plushy cushions as a boy? Or to run and awaken his father in the morning?

Once again, Rolf was hit with the magnitude of what had been stolen from them all.

"You remind me of someone," the king said. Rolf looked up to find the king studying him once again, his head tilted slightly to the side.

"My father–"

"No, it's not that," the king interrupted him. "It's something else. I didn't realize until you shared your story about the deer, though..." He drew in a shuddering breath. "You remind me," he said slowly, "of my wife."

Rolf had not expected that. Nor had he expected the gentle caress with which the king used for her.

"If you please, Your Majesty," Rolf said, trying to control his voice. "What happened? Why is the queen locked away in a tower?"

The king stood and went to the window. "I shouldn't tell you this. But for some reason...for some reason, I feel I should." He sighed and shook his head. "When my son was small, she took him to the menagerie. It was not a place I liked for her to go often. More wooded and difficult to defend. But she loved it. It...it quieted her soul." He shook his head again. "The day of my son's sixth birthday, she took him there after the celebration to rest, despite my instructions to go straight home. I should have taken them there myself. I should have..." The king's voice grew tight and low. "They both fell asleep there, and an animal attacked him. I never..." The king was crying now, tears running down his face as his voice broke. "I wish you could have seen him. He was the most beautiful little boy. And clever. And..." He closed his eyes and covered them with his hand. "To see what was left of his body mangled and bloody..."

Rolf squeezed his own eyes shut. He wanted desperately to tell his father who he was, to relieve his pain and to beg him to release his mother. But the time wasn't right. Not yet.

"So…" Rolf had to clear his throat twice. "The queen was blamed."

"Charged with negligence," the king whispered.

"Did you agree with that charge?" Rolf asked. Anger and desire warred within him as he wanted to embrace and shout at his father all at the same time.

The king shrugged. "It was expected of me. I had warned her, after all, not to go to the menagerie. A new animal had been brought in, and the keeper hadn't yet decided if the conditions were safe. My advisers. The court. Even the lawyers said…" He let out a gusty sigh. "She never argued. Something inside her died that day. And she's never uttered so much as peep in her own favor."

Audacity streaked through Rolf. It wasn't an appropriate question. But he needed to know. "Did you love her?"

For a moment, he wondered if the king would order him out. Or possibly have him beheaded. But the king only turned enough to smile at him sadly. "She is dearer to me than my own life."

"Something died inside you that day, too. Didn't it?" Rolf asked, his voice nearly a whisper.

The king absently stroked the edge of the sheath he wore at his belt. "There has been no life in me for a long time."

The silence was suddenly deafening, and Rolf had to squeeze his eyes shut again to keep the tears inside.

This father had never wanted to punish his mother. Unlike the proud King Albert that Tobias and the faerie had painted in his head, this man was broken.

"But none of this is your burden to bear," the king said kindly, coming to sit on the chair opposite Rolf's before the fire. "Tell me. What can I do for you? How can we seek justice for you?"

Rolf stared at his father, his mind suddenly like a swirling maelstrom over the sea.

He had a plan.

The garden. It all came back to the garden. The place where the atrocity had begun would be the place where it ended. The plan was risky. Tobias would see to that. There was too much magic involved for it to be otherwise. Magic that wasn't subject to Rolf's wishes. But if there was any way... Rolf looked at his father once again.

"I told you," Rolf said slowly, "that my father used to work here."

The king nodded. "Yes? What about it?"

Rolf took a steadying breath. "What if I told you that this castle was where I was taken from my parents, too?"

The king froze. "But...surely I would have heard."

"From what I understand," Rolf continued, "it happened around the time of the incident with the prince."

The king's eyes were suddenly too wide and too bright. But he nodded. "And...and you think you can find justice here?"

Rolf nodded, his sorrow hardening into resolve. "I think I can. But I'll need your help."

CHAPTER
TWENTY-ONE

Rolf waited in the menagerie, seconds passing like eons. The moon was hidden behind clouds, which made the scene all the more foreboding, and explosions of lightning exploded in the distance, thunder rumbling across the distant hills. For the thousandth time that night, Rolf touched the ring, and he prayed that if Tobias somehow bested him, the faerie would find a way to keep her goddaughter safe.

He walked in circles as he waited, arguing with himself about what might go wrong. It was dangerous. There was no question about that. He could use magic wishes, of course, but he still had no idea how many of Tobias's charms were hovering nearby, or how many of them might be set off if he accessed his wishes.

The king had offered to send guards with Rolf to arrest his captor, should he appear, but Rolf had begged him to have them wait in the shadows. Tobias was too clever to appear if he felt he was at a disadvantage. And if he wasn't at a disadvantage, if he had gotten more dangerous charms that day, the guards' lives would be forfeit. No, Rolf had to do this alone. Without magic.

And pray it turned out for the best.

"So," a deep voice called from the darkness. "You've decided to come to me like a man." In a flash of lightning, Rolf caught a glimpse of a big man coming toward him. And though he couldn't make out details above the man's silhouette, it was one he knew without question.

"I'm not the one coward enough to abduct children and then let a woman take the fall for my crime," Rolf retorted.

Tobias chuckled. "Surely you know I have half a dozen charms hovering over this place now. And twice that waiting to pounce on the girl once you're done."

Rolf clenched his fists, forcing himself not to leap at the man. Time. He needed to give Tobias time.

"And yes, I know she's trapped in your ring."

Rolf had been breathing evenly enough so far. But at these words, his heart stopped.

"Boy," Tobias said with a sneer, visible in another flash of lightning, "I raised you. I know everything about you and your foolish little bird." As he spoke, Rolf noticed a strange sort of dark smoke hovering in the air above them. It only took him a few seconds to realize that Tobias's charms were about to take hold. It seemed that these charms didn't even need his magic to begin. They weren't reactive. They were meant to attack.

"Poetic, isn't it?" Tobias called above the approaching

storm. "What began here will end here. But I suppose that's why you chose this place."

"My mother fell here!" Rolf shouted, largely for the sake of incriminating Tobias, but also because he felt like it. "Now it's your turn!"

"The queen deserved everything she got and more! Gifted with a child who could have given her *anything* she wished. And what did she do? She hid him away! How much good could you have done for this kingdom? You could have ended poverty and starvation. And instead, she kept you to herself!"

"Don't pretend you're interested in philanthropy," Rolf snarled. "My mother tried to protect me! And to protect the kingdom from me!"

"And now you want justice. How do you plan to bring that about?" Tobias laughed. "You tried wishing away my charms, but that failed. I'm not sure what the point is in trying again." He raised his arm, another charm glowing visibly in his hand. "But I do thank you. It created the perfect opportunity for me to finish this neatly." He raised the charm higher.

"You're right," Rolf called back. "My magic can't rival yours."

In the light of the charms hovering above them, thick clouds of smoky light, Rolf could see the confusion on Tobias's face. And in spite of himself, Rolf grinned.

"Then what–" Tobias began, but in one swift movement, Rolf drew the sword from his hip.

"This." And with that, he leaped forward and plunged the sword into the man's heart.

The charms surrounding them began to crackle, smoke making the air nearly unbreathable. Rolf could feel the magic building in the air. A small bolt of purple light, similar to a miniature lightning strike, moved from the charm in Tobias's unclenched hand down the man's body and up Rolf's sword into his own hands. Rolf tried to abandon the sword in the dead man's chest to run. But his fingers wouldn't let go.

Rolf was stuck.

"Run!" he shouted at the people he could hear behind him, for his witnesses had begun pouring out of every corner and shadow available. Guards called out to one another, and he could hear his father shouting his name.

"It's not safe!" Rolf cried over his shoulder, still trying to pry his hands from the weapon. "Get away!"

"Rolf!" His father's voice was suddenly near hum. In a flash of lightning, Rolf could see his father appear on his right. "Let the sword go! It's not worth it!"

"I can't!" Rolf tugged in vain again. "I'm stuck!"

The king put his large, weathered hands over Rolf's and tried to pull his hands off the sword. But it was as though Rolf had become one with the weapon.

"You have to go!" Rolf said, looking back up at the magic above them, which was swirling faster and faster. "The magic will kill us both!" Then he remembered. "Please! Take the ring from my right hand! Give the ring to the faerie—"

"I'm not leaving you!" the king shouted over the boom of thunder. "I'm not losing my boy again!"

The charms that had been circling above them were now moving so quickly they were simply continual flashes of light. Rolf squeezed his eyes shut and prepared himself for the final explosion. But rather than pain, he felt his father take his face and press it against his chest, his large arms covering Rolf's head as a shield.

The next few moments felt like an eternity as the magic continued to crackle and smoke, and the air felt as though it was ready to burst into flames.

But then it didn't.

CHAPTER
TWENTY-TWO

Instead, droplets began to fall. More and more droplets until Rolf opened his eyes to see a rain unlike any other. Each droplet was filled with soft blue magic light. And like the rain, a new light began to descend. And as the water hit his hands, they were gently released from the sword's hilt.

Rolf pulled away from his father to watch the faerie who landed on the grass beside them. His father, too, looked up and gasped as she smiled.

"Well done, Prince Rolf." Her smile widened as she looked up. "Not only did you find a way to bring about justice, but you enticed him to gather all the remaining charms together so I could destroy them at once." She beamed. "Excellent."

Rolf took a deep breath of the clean air. It smelled of water and earth, all traces of Tobias's purchased magic gone.

"The question remains," the faerie was now looking at the king as she spoke. "Now that you know the truth, what will you do?"

The king stared at her for a long moment before he turned and began to run toward the castle.

"That," said the faerie with another smile, "won't be necessary." She waved her wand, and Rolf's mother appeared beside them. For a moment, she looked like she might pass out. But then she spotted Rolf. And without question or hesitation, put her hands on his face and drew it down to hers.

"My son," she whispered over and over again, pressing her forehead against his. "My son. I'm so sorry!"

"The second question remains," the faerie said, turning to Rolf. His mother let him stand but wrapped her arms around him. Rolf's father wrapped his arms around both of them. "What are you going to do now that justice has been restored?"

Rolf immediately removed the ring from his finger. After turning in his hands for a moment, he put it on the grass in front of him. It shone in the moonlight as the clouds drifted away.

"I wish," he said in a trembling voice, "that Bethan was free again."

In a swirl of smoke, Bethan appeared. She looked around her wildly until her gaze settled on Rolf. She leaped into his arms and held on tight.

"I was so afraid," she whispered in his ear. "He wanted to kill–"

"We don't have to be afraid anymore." Rolf gently pried her arms off and took a step back so they were holding hands. His stomach roiled within him as he took a steadying breath and prepared himself for what he had to do.

Bethan followed his pointed gaze down to where Tobias's still form lay, and she gasped. "You mean... we're free?" she whispered.

"Almost." Rolf did his best to smile, but his voice cracked.

"What..." she shook her head. "I don't understand."

"Bethan," Rolf said, taking her face in his hands. "What I did to you—"

"You didn't know." Bethan vehemently shook her head. "You were a child."

Rolf nodded, but he could keep up his smile no longer. "I know. But nothing...nothing I say or do will ever make up for the time you lost or the suffering your family endured because of me."

Bethan's gaze narrowed. "You know I don't hold that against you."

"So," Rolf continued, "I'm going to make three wishes. And the first two are for you."

"Rolf—"

He drew her closed and gently kissed her forehead. "I wish," he said, his lips brushing her skin, "that you live a long and happy life."

"Rolf!"

"That your family be rich and well-fed."

"Rolf, you listen to me—"

215

"And that you find a man who loves you more than life and gives you all the children and happiness you desire."

"What are you doing?" her voice rose as she grasped his arms tightly.

"What I should have done long ago."

"No! Wait, you can't–"

"I must." He kissed her temple, his lips wanting nothing more than to linger, soaking in the warmth of her skin. But unlike when he had proposed, Rolf finally understood love. Letting go of her, he forced himself to step back.

"I wish," he said, staring into her eyes for the last time, each word more painful than the last, "that you were home."

Bethan began to cry and protest as he stepped back and forced his hands to drop hers. And then, in a swirl of smoke, she was gone.

His mother was the first to his side. Rob scrunched his eyes shut as the pain in his chest flared. He felt his mother's soft hands on his arms as she drew him close. Then his father's hand was on his shoulder, squeezing it tightly.

"You said you had three wishes," the faerie said softly. "What is the last?"

Rolf forced his eyes open. "I wish," he said carefully. "To be rid of my gift."

His mother gasped, but he kept his eyes on the faerie. She studied him for a moment. Finally, the corner of her mouth quirked up.

"Very well," she said, taking a step back. "Your wish is granted." She lifted her wand and waved it at him once. Twice. Three times.

Smoke surrounded him once again. But instead of filling his body as it always had, he felt empty. The constant crackle of magic that he had always known began to leak out of him. Rolf stumbled slightly, his parents catching him as magic light poured from his body back into the faerie's wand. As he felt the last of it leave him, he fell to his knees, breathing hard as he tried to catch his breath.

"I'm curious," the faerie asked, taking a step closer. "You could have had anything in the world that you desired. You could have been the richest king and the most powerful monarch. Your kingship could have—"

"Because," Rolf gasped, struggling to right himself, "no mere man was meant to have that kind of power."

The faerie stared at him before giving him a soft smile. "Then you have learned what your fathers did not."

Rolf looked up at his own father. But instead of looking shocked or angry, his father simply bowed his head.

"I do wish," Rolf said, getting slowly to his feet, "that you would continue to watch over Bethan. And...make sure that she's safe and happy."

The faerie arched a brow. "Is that a wish?"

Rolf gave her a tired smile and inclined his head. "A humble request."

The faerie began to rise into the air. Rolf heard the gasps of the guards around them, but he kept his eyes on her. "Then that wish," she said, "I will most happily grant."

CHAPTER
TWENTY-THREE

Though the man who had started everything was gone, the excitement was hardly over. The very next day, the king sent out a plea to the faerie court to help them catch the dark faerie who had sold Tobias all of his charms. And though the faerie courts, Rolf was told, usually didn't deign to mix themselves into human politics, the waves created by this particular dark faerie seemed enough to garner their attention, particularly when word came out that Healanie testified to what he had been done, and how she had spent weeks chasing the traveling charms all around the countryside, trying to destroy them.

When the dark wizard was brought to heel, however, Rolf was more than a little surprised to see Josif brought in with him.

"Is this pathetic being in need of punishment as well?" The towering male faerie acting as a guard shoved the thin man forward so hard he nearly stumbled. "He was found in the kidnapper's old home."

"No!" Rolf hurried forward to give Josif his arm, as the poor man seemed on the verge of fainting. "No, he was another victim as well."

For a moment, he wasn't sure the faerie guard would agree with him based on the look of disgust the tall faerie cast down upon the cowering man. But to Rolf's relief, in the end, the faerie court took only the dark faerie for punishment. When Rolf's father learned who Josif was, he seemed equally disposed to punish the man. But Rolf would not budge on his insistence that Josif had saved him more than once, and in the end, Josif was delighted to receive a job in the stables.

"You're sure I can't find you something easier?" Rolf asked with a frown. Josif was rather frail and no longer young.

Josif beamed. "Naw. Always want'd someth'n of mine own to boast." He stood taller. "Earnin' m'way. Best it could be." And though Rolf hardly thought a steady wage was enough for what Josif had done, he had to finally allow that it was Josif's decision to be made.

More importantly, Rolf's mother was cleared of all wrongdoing in the presence of the courts and the people. And thanks to Rolf's testimony of things he had seen during his unconscious dream-state, very little pressure was needed to coerce the guilty parties who had testified against the queen to admit their lies as well. A particularly nasty courtier named Lady Chrysanthemum was stripped of her

THE PRINCE'S DANGEROUS WISH

title and placed in the dungeon for her false testimony against Queen Nadine, and several other courtiers admitted to doing the same.

Rolf watched the proceedings as though he were on the outside looking in. Though his place was always at his father's right hand, he felt like he was floating above the spectacle, similar to what he had done during his two-year dream. The whole ordeal felt as though it was happening to someone else, and he was only borrowing a body from which to look on. And though he knew he should be ecstatic at his mother's vindication, he felt strangely numb.

The quiet moments, the ones with his parents, felt far more real. Probably because their pain was so similar to his own. His mother moved back into her old rooms and was assigned a full brigade of personal servants once again. Over the next few months, Rolf was relieved to see her gain some weight again, as she had been a wisp of nothing when he returned. Color came back into her cheeks, and her gait became stronger and surer once again.

But the spark he remembered in her eyes from when he was a boy seemed to have been extinguished. She could smile whenever it was expected of her, but Rolf didn't miss the haunted look that filled her eyes whenever she thought no one was looking.

After two months of this, Rolf finally grew anxious enough to ask his father about it. They were riding horseback through fields of corn. The wind was blowing colder, and the servants working the fields raced to get the harvest in as a storm approached from the western shores.

BRITTANY FICHTER

"Your mother was always...different," his father said, his brow furrowing as he stared into the storm. "I married her because she was so different from the other girls. Nadine... Nadine was real." He smiled a little. "Her mother had beat her into submission, trying to make her into what would be the perfect princess. I knew this and somehow convinced myself that she would be far happier as a true princess." He stretched his arm out toward the castle in the distance. "All the riches she could wish for. Homage required by the women who had once despised her." He sighed. "But, as it turned out, I was no better than her mother. In fact, I was worse."

"So she wasn't happy the way I remember, then?" Rolf asked.

"Oh, no. She was very happy." His father gave him a gentle smile. "When she was with you."

"And...you really never knew I was gifted?"

The king shook his head. "She told everyone that you were sickly. I was confused by this, as you had been strong from the day you were born. But I let her have her way." His face darkened. "Until the day of your birthday."

"You couldn't have known I would reveal my gift," Rolf said. "Or that the worst person in the castle would be watching."

His father shook his head again. "It doesn't matter. Your mother, while not what everyone expected, was a woman of sense. I should have listened to her. If I had from the start, she would never have felt the need to hide your gift from me." He looked down.

Rolf stared at him for a long moment. The silver ring with the pink gem flower, which he still wore on his smallest finger, seemed to burn against his skin. The wind began to whip, making it harder to hear, so he moved his horse closer to his father's. "I think you should tell her," he called over the noise.

"Tell her?" his father echoed.

Rolf nodded. "All of it. What you just told me." His throat felt suddenly restricted. "Don't let her feel alone anymore."

His father gazed at him for a moment. "Are we talking about your mother?" he asked. "Or someone else?"

Rolf swallowed hard and touched his heels to his horse's side. "I want to go look at the bay before the storm hits," he called over his shoulder. And he left his father to follow behind him.

That night, Rolf went to his mother's room to ask her a question, but as he raised his hand to knock, he realized he could hear voices coming from within. He paused and put his ear to the door, ignoring the guards' quizzical looks. If growing up with Tobias had taught him anything, it was that there were very few souls for whom Rolf worried about their opinion of him.

He smiled and dropped his hand a moment later when he heard his father say something incoherent, and his mother laughed. Turning around, he went back to his own chambers. He could ask her in the morning.

THINGS WERE BETTER AFTER THAT. Rolf had daily training sessions with his father and the kingdom's best swords masters. Miraculously, he hadn't wasted away completely during his two-year sleep, but his strength certainly hadn't been what it was before the sleep. And even before that time, he had never been unusually strong.

With his father's help, however, and his trainers' guidance, he began to feel like he was returning to life. He grew stronger, and soon had a new daily routine of his own. A dozen times a day, he said a prayer of thanks for Bethan and how she had encouraged him to learn to do things on his own, rather than wishing them done. For now that he couldn't wish anything away, he was faced with a load of tasks that threatened to eat him alive every day.

His father had been pleasantly surprised by all that Rolf knew, thanks to his long sleep, and had immediately begun to give him tasks that would one day prepare him for the throne. Rolf stumbled into bed each night, hardly conscious enough to undress. He didn't mind, though. The crushing load of burdens kept his mind too occupied to spend hours thinking about her.

And yet, he did think of her. In everything he did, she was there. He could hear her voice teasing him to try again each time he lost a sword match. He could hear her quiet compassion when he listened to the problems brought by his people every day. He heard her praise each time he learned to do something new. And it was torture. Torture he wouldn't trade for anything else in the world.

"Rolf."

Rolf looked up from the law he had tried to read and gotten lost in three times. When he saw who it was, he stood. "Mother. To what do I owe this pleasure?"

His mother, who was looking far more like the happy young woman he remembered, touched his cheek. Her eyes, no longer so distant or longing, now probed his, and he suddenly felt quite exposed.

"You're unhappy," she finally said, retiring to the chair on the opposite side of his writing table.

Rolf tried to force a smile as he returned to his own seat. "I'm home. This is the happiest I've ever been."

But she just shook her head. "I don't think so." Then she laughed ruefully. "Rolf, I have been pretending since the moment I could first stand. Don't think I don't know what it looks like when you smile, but all you want to do is cry."

Rolf didn't know what to say to this. He looked back down at the parchment in front of him, but none of the words made sense anymore.

"Do you know where she is?" she asked quietly.

Rolf's throat tightened, and he closed his eyes and shook his head. He heard her sigh.

"And you're sure sending her back was the right thing?"

Rolf drew in a deep breath and then leaned his head back to stare up at the ceiling. "It's all she ever wanted."

"I saw the way she looked at you that night you sent her home. And I don't believe that either."

He looked at her and raised one brow. "You could read her mind?"

"No." She slapped his arm playfully. "I know what it looks like to be in love."

Rolf swallowed hard. "She loved me as a playmate. A brother. Nothing more."

His mother stood and went to the window. "For being so brilliant, you and your father really are quite dull sometimes."

"I proposed to her, Mother. She turned me down."

"Yes, as you've said. And that was what? More than two years ago?"

He pushed the parchment away and leaned on his writing table. "For most of which I was asleep."

"If that makes you think—"

"Mother."

His voice must have betrayed him because she turned and looked at him again. This time, there was no smile in her eyes.

"I kidnapped a little girl." Rolf looked up at her, challenging her to disagree with him. "And I held her against her will. For thirteen years, I kept her. She nearly died because of me." Hatred for himself flared in a way it hadn't in a long time, and he pulled the silver ring off his smallest finger and squeezed it until the gems dug into his skin and his fingers hurt. "I had no right to keep her any longer. And I'm not about to go gallivanting around the world to find her and take her away from all she left behind once again."

"You didn't ask her what she wanted," his mother said in a small voice.

Rolf shook his head. "She'd been asking all her life. I just didn't listen."

His mother went to him once more and began to comb his hair with her fingers.

"I didn't live what you did. And...as a mother, it kills me that I didn't protect you from it."

"Mother, there was no way you could have—"

"But I will tell you this. I was the girl who was in love. And the man I loved didn't listen. He thought I wanted the world. Fame and fortune and fine silks and all the rest." Rolf's mother gently took his chin in her hands and lifted it so he had to look up at her. "All I wanted was him. But he never thought to ask."

THE QUEEN'S words continued to haunt Rolf after that.

On one hand, they brought him joy every time he saw his parents together. His mother was still quite fragile, But, as though to match her, the king had undeniably become quite gentle. Often, he caught them gazing into one another's eyes, and the light that had left his mother's face was beginning to return.

On the other hand, it made him more aware than ever that he was alone.

Two weeks after his conversation with his mother, Rolf

was standing at his father's side, listening to the complaints of the citizens who came to seek aid. Even now, it was strange to stand on this side of the throne room. Still, it was one of his favorite duties. He could no longer wish problems out of existence. But he was the crown prince of a powerful kingdom. If this was how he could atone for—

The man at the front of the line had just come forward and opened his mouth to speak, but he was interrupted by a commotion coming from the back of the line. People cried out in protest as a young woman marched in, guards on her tail.

"What is this?" the king asked, frowning as he rose from his throne. But when the young woman threw the hood of her dusty cloak off, Rolf's breath left him.

"You!" she shouted at Rolf, her blue eyes blazing as her voice rang clearly through the throne room. Then, for some reason, she faltered, looking around her for the first time, as if suddenly realizing where she was. As she hesitated, two guards took hold of her arms.

Rolf found his voice.

"Wait!" he shouted. The guards looked at him as though he'd lost his mind, but instead, he only descended the steps, feeling very much as though he was in a dream. Glancing at one another, the guards let go and backed away again as Rolf walked slowly down the red carpet toward her.

Her hair was mussed from the hood, and her clothes were covered in dust. Her shoes were worn, and one had a hole in the toe, but her eyes blazed as brightly as ever.

As he drew near, she seemed on the verge of losing her nerve, her gaze traveling up and down his person twice.

"I believe," Rolf managed to say, "you had something you wanted to say to me?"

At this, her eyes burned again. "Yes." She swallowed and lifted her chin. "I came all the way here to say that I want my ring."

He blinked at her. "You...want the ring you were trapped in for days?"

"Yes. Yes, I do. And you had no right to take it from me."

Unable to help himself, Rolf took her hands in his. They were rougher than he remembered, but that only made him want to kiss them more.

"I thought you wanted to go home," he said slowly.

"I did." She glanced up and down his person again. "But...I can want more than one thing at a time."

Stepping closer, until their faces were only inches apart, Rolf looked down at the beautiful girl he'd dreamed of every night since she had left.

"And what do you want, Bethan?" His voice came out huskier than usual.

"I told you. I want my ring." She held his gaze steadily, though her breathing hitched slightly.

"You know," he said, letting go of her hands to slide the ring from his finger, "this ring comes at a price."

Her voice quivered slightly. "And what would that be?"

He held the ring up between them. "Me. And before you answer, you should know that I come with a lifetime of servitude. A castle to defend. People to watch over. Justice to mete."

She looked longingly at the ring and then back up at him. "Do you think it's a price I'm not rich enough to pay?"

Unable to keep the charade, Rolf closed his eyes and let his head rest against hers. "Bethan," he whispered, breathing deeply her familiar scent. "I don't deserve you."

"I think that's for me to decide," she said stubbornly. "Now, where's my ring?"

Laughing as tears ran down his cheeks, Rolf took the ring and slipped it onto her finger. Then, unable to hold back any longer, he cupped her jaw in his hands and drew her mouth to his. And as she threw her arms around his neck, a cheer went up from everyone around them.

But to Rolf, for all he knew, they were standing by a waterfall, washed in the light of a silver moon once more.

CHAPTER
TWENTY-FOUR

Bethan's family, with Healanie's assistance, had accompanied her to the capital city to find Rolf. Though they were less than enthusiastic at first that she wanted to return to the boy who had taken her, a good word from the faerie had somewhat calmed their fears. The discovery that he was their crown prince did even more.

Bethan and Rolf were to be married a month later. Upon announcement of Bethan's return, Rolf's mother glowed in a way he had never seen her, even as a boy, and his father looked as though he might burst with pride.

"You're sure they don't mind that I'm a commoner?" she asked several days before the wedding.

Rolf laughed and kissed her on the cheek. Then on the mouth for good measure. They were walking in his mother's favorite garden, and Bethan was looking radiant but worried.

"My mother has already decided that you're her favorite

child," he chuckled. "And my father just wants grandchildren. I don't think he cares how he gets them." He took her hand and pressed it against his lips before holding it against his chest. "I have to ask, though." He took a deep breath. "Why? Why did you want to come back for me?"

"Are you still worried about that?" She shook her head at the ground. "The fact that I convinced my faerie godmother to help us traverse all the way across the kingdom should be enough to convince you–"

"It's...not that." He brushed a strand of hair out of her face. "I want to know why."

She walked over to a lookout that provided an excellent view of the ocean. He followed her and waited, knowing that she would speak when she was ready.

"I was happy to see my family again," she finally said, her words slow and deliberate. "But the longer I was home, the more I realized that I wasn't where I was supposed to be."

"You were exactly where you were supposed to be," he said, coming to stand behind her and wrapping his arms around her shoulders.

She shook her head. "When Healanie told me how she had given you the gift in order to teach you what your forefathers had failed to learn..." She huffed. "I'll admit that I'm probably one of the few people stupid enough to shout at a faerie and survive the encounter without an extra horn or some sort of awful curse."

"You would look adorable with a horn. Like a bright-eyed little unicorn."

She elbowed him in the ribs but turned a slight shade of pink. "You know what I mean. Anyway, I demanded to know why she had allowed you to fall into Tobias's hands. And why she had let you take me."

"And what did she say?" Rolf asked, his throat suddenly thick.

"She said...that what had happened to you would bless your kingdom for generations. But that you had needed a light in the dark."

"You were always my light," Rolf said, holding her just a little tighter.

Bethan turned in his arms and faced him. "And you," she said "were my knight."

He frowned down at her. "How so?"

"You never stopped fighting. You were absolutely ignorant of the world in every way possible. But you sought to learn. And to try. And to fight the walls with which Tobias tried to cage you." She paused to straighten Rolf's cloak. "You might not have seen the world for what it was. But you always fought to do what was right. And when I found myself without that..." She shrugged then met his eyes. "I felt utterly alone."

Rolf pulled her closer and had just touched his lips to hers when someone let out a cry behind him.

"Rolf, for shame! You'll scandalize the whole castle." His mother did not sound scandalized at all. "You can have your bride in three days. Come, Bethan. We have another fitting to do." She held her hand out, and Bethan, flushed again, took it with a shy smile.

"I told you you were her favorite child," Rold called after them.

"Of course," his mother called back, unabashed. "You're not nearly as pretty as she is."

Rolf chuckled to himself and turned back to look out at the ocean as the sun began to set.

"I've never seen her so happy."

Rolf looked up to see Alicia come to stand behind him.

"I'm glad to hear that," Rolf said.

She smiled at him. "I can't believe I'm saying this, but... maybe that faerie did know what she was doing after all."

Rolf just smiled back. But in his heart, he knew he couldn't agree more.

CHAPTER
TWENTY-FIVE

Nadine frowned at her reflection in the mirror. "I shouldn't be this anxious."

"It's your first public appearance since the trial," Alicia mumbled, her mouth full of hairpins. "It only makes sense for you to be anxious."

Nadine sighed and turned her head to examine Alicia's work. As always, it was perfect. Ringlets had been expertly placed in the latest fashion, and flowers matching the ones chosen for the wedding were woven in and out of her curls.

Nadine's dress was no less stunning. While far more subdued than usual, as it wouldn't do to try to outshine the bride, it was a deep purple with subtle flounces making it swirl gracefully whenever she turned. And though there were more lines at the corners of her eyes and mouth than she remembered, and her skin hadn't yet recovered its full color after the years in her tower, Nadine felt surprisingly put together. On the outside, that was.

239

But inside, she was just as terrified as she had ever been. Or rather, more so. And with a generous amount of guilt, she realized that she wished her son's wedding was already over.

For years, Nadine had excelled at exuding perfection upon command. It didn't last, of course. She always grew tired quickly when she had to prance around on display for royal events such as this. But her carefully crafted mask seemed to have cracked during her years of captivity. And now, everyone in court would see the true queen for the first time.

Nadine wanted no part of it.

"Come," Alicia said gently. "The guests are beginning to arrive."

With a sigh, Nadine nodded and made her way out of her chambers and to the place where the wedding party was preparing. She felt as though every eye in the castle was on her. That was ridiculous, of course, as Nadine wasn't the one getting married. But she was the once-convicted queen. And as far as attention went, that was far worse.

"Your Highness?"

Nadine stopped as a woman about fifteen years her senior stopped before her and curtsied deeply.

"Melisa, good morning!" she said as her son's future mother-in-law rose.

"Your Highness, I'm so sorry to ask this of you. I'm sure you're very busy, but..." The woman, who had never seemed anything less than the perfect picture of confidence, sighed and pursed her lips.

"What is it?" Nadine asked, genuinely curious now.

"It's my daughter," Melisa said. "She's...she's very anxious."

"About what?" Nadine asked. "Is something wrong?" She began running through a mental list of all the things that might have possibly gone wrong.

"No, nothing is wrong," Melisa said with a weak smile. "She's...she's anxious, though. And nothing I say or do seems to help."

Full understanding dawned on Nadine. And for once, she understood perfectly.

"Where is she?" she asked with a sad smile. "Let me see her."

When Nadine was ushered into the bridal chambers, she found Bethan pacing the room, and for some reason, she was startled by the girl's youth. Had she really been younger than this child when she was married?

"Bethan?" she asked gently.

At the sound of her voice, however, Bethan stood still and looked up. And on her lovely face was an expression Nadine knew all too well. Without waiting for the girl to speak, she went to her and drew her into a tight embrace, which tightened as she remembered how much she had wanted someone to do this for her the day she got married.

"I'm sorry, Your Highness," Bethan said, wiping the corners of her eyes. "I don't know what's wrong with me. For some reason, I've only now realized the...the *weight* of what I'm about to do and become and—"

"Bethan," Nadine said, putting her hands on the girl's face. "It's all right."

Bethan sucked in a sharp breath and seemed to really focus on the queen for the first time. "It is?" she asked in a quavering voice.

Nadine gave her a sad smile and nodded. "I'm not saying it won't be hard. It is hard. Every day is hard. But...you'll be doing it all with your closest friend."

At this, Bethan smiled slightly.

"And," Nadine said, pulling her into another embrace, "you won't be doing it alone. I swear it." And Nadine meant every word. Bethan was exactly the kind of girl she would have wished for her son. And in no way did Nadine mean to leave her daughter-in-law the way her mother-in-law had abandoned and then simply observed her.

Bethan's arms tightened around her. "Thank you," she whispered. "That's all I needed to hear."

NADINE's own wedding had been expensive and grandiose. And while Bethan and Rolf's wedding wasn't cheap by any standard, it was far simpler and far more to Bethans's—and Nadine's—taste. This had, of course, enraged Nadine's mother-in-law, which was more than fine by Nadine. And once Nadine was seated on the throne behind her husband, where they could see the ceremony unfold, she decided that it was the most beautiful wedding she had ever witnessed.

The flowers and silken decorations were lovely, of course. But most importantly, Nadine was watching her beloved boy, the one she'd believed lost to her forever, smile radiantly as he pledged himself to the girl he loved. She glanced over at her husband, expecting to see him smiling. But to her surprise, he was frowning down at the ceremony below.

What had perturbed him?

His frown briefly disappeared as he boomed his pronouncement over the couple once their vows were finished, but then it returned once they were seated to eat and watch the celebration.

Hoping to distract her husband, Nadine ventured quietly, "She'll be a good queen."

Albert nodded, but it was her mother-in-law who spoke. "And how would you know what that is?"

A sharp pang of shame and embarrassment made Nadine instinctively bow her head. To her surprise, though, her husband's voice was suddenly just as acidic.

"And you will keep a civil tongue in your head when you speak to my wife." He never raised his voice, but the sharpness of his words was evident in the look of disgust and outrage on his mother's face.

"Nadine," he said, still glaring at his mother as he stood. "Would you join me for a word?"

Fear and anxiety rolled around in Nadine's stomach as, holding her hand on his arm, he led her outside. It was the same tone of voice he had used the day he'd found her in the menagerie on her birthday.

"You're unhappy," Nadine said as soon as they were out on the balcony alone. "What can I—"

"I'm sorry."

Nadine blinked at him. "You're...what?"

"I'm sorry," he said again. "For everything." As he spoke, his voice grew tight. "For not escorting you home myself the night of his party. For the sentencing. For not asking or listening. I'm sorry for...for it all."

"But Albert," Nadine said with a slight frown. "You've already apologized."

"Not the way I need to," he said. "Because I need you not only to know what a nightmare it was to lock you up, but how I've wanted to die every day since." He took her hand and held it in his own. "I've regretted every day of my life for the past thirteen years, and while I'm coming to terms with the understanding that I'll never forgive myself—"

"But...I forgive you," Nadine said softly.

He stared at her as though she'd grown a second nose. "You...you what?"

She smiled and touched his face. "I forgive you."

His hand reached up to touch hers, and Nadine drank in the physical contact as though she'd never felt it before.

The last month had been better. Albert had fully admitted to his sins and had become far more engaged with seeing to her health often. The man she had loved for so long—loved and feared he would love another in her absence—still cared for her. But that had been most of what he had done since Rolf had come back, handling her with care, as though she were a delicate little glass bird.

Nadine didn't dare to say it for fear it would be denied her, but what she wanted...the man she wanted was the one she had been forced to leave behind.

That man, however, seemed to be gone. Rolf told her once that Albert had described it as though he had died inside when he lost his family. And Nadine mourned the loss of that man, for she had loved him dearly.

This man, though, the one holding onto her hand as though it might save his life, was one she would like very much to know.

"I wasn't perfect either if you recall," Nadine said shyly. "I didn't listen when you told me to avoid the menagerie."

He huffed. "You wouldn't have needed to if I had simply gone with you."

"No, but..." She paused. "You mustn't talk of the old days as if they were all bad."

"Oh really?" he huffed.

She smiled. "I was very happy once. When Rolf was small, and you would come to see us, away from all the courtiers and the spying eyes..." She shrugged as a new hope blossomed within her. "And I'd like...I'd like to be that happy again."

She had been planning on listing all of her imperfections so her husband might not feel so alone. But before she could utter one of them, her husband's mouth was on hers, and he was drawing her near. The warmth of his chest felt like the sun as it seemed to touch every corner of her soul that had been frozen for the last...well, for all her life.

She had never felt so alive before.

A cheer went up from within, and they smiled at one another and made their way to the balcony opening, where they could see their son and his bride being showered by rose petals as the blessings of their friends were being shouted aloud around them. Nadine leaned her head against her husband's chest as she watched with a smile.

And for the first time in her life, she knew with full confidence that she was exactly where and who she needed to be.

EPILOGUE

Alicia appeared out in the corridor, where Rolf's father was trying to convince him not to panic. His wife's screams had terrified him more than anything he had ever heard, even in his most vivid nightmares, and Rolf was on the verge of breaking down the door. Now he stared at his mother's best friend, wanting desperately to ask after Bethan's health, but the words were stuck in his throat. The smile on Alicia's face, however, made the awful question unnecessary. She beamed at him. "She's ready to see you now."

Rolf hurried so fast he nearly stumbled into his wife's bedroom. Maidservants were opening windows and quickly gathering the last of a pile of soiled towels before scurrying out of the room.

"Only a few minutes," Rolf's mother said, touching him on the shoulder. "She's tired and needs sleep." Then she closed the door behind her, and Rolf was finally alone with his wife and their new child.

"How are you?" he asked, sitting slowly on the edge of the bed. Bethan's face was covered in a sheen of sweat, and her eyes were red and had dark circles beneath them. But the smile on her face was beautiful. And in her arms lay a bundle wrapped in the finest of embroidered swaddling cloths.

"A girl," Bethan whispered, looking down at their child. "We have a girl." Then her eyes darted up to his. "You don't think your parents—"

"I'm glad it's a girl," Rolf said firmly. "And so will be everyone else who matters." He looked back down at the small bundle. A tiny round head covered in honey-blond hair was barely visible over the swaths of cloth surrounding her. Rolf folded the cloths back to see a little face that took his breath away.

About half a year after their wedding, Bethan had come to him, her eyes sparkling and her breath slightly too fast.

"What is it?" he'd asked, putting down his pen. She opened her mouth twice to speak, but both times, had closed it again. Then she had simply taken one of his hands and placed it on her belly.

Rolf had been living on pins and needles ever since.

"Bethan, she's beautiful," he whispered now. Then he looked at his wife and kissed her temple. "I'm so proud of you." He looked back down at the little eyes, which were squeezed shut. "What do you think we should name her?"

Before she could respond, the room filled with smoke, and Healanie appeared at the foot of the bed.

Bethan beamed, but Rolf felt his blood run cold.

"You made it!" Bethan cried.

"Let me see," the faerie cooed, hurrying to stand across from Rolf on the other side of the bed. Rolf sat frozen, wanting nothing more than to scoop up his wife and his child and run and hide. But he knew better than to try. So, quite unwillingly, he handed their child back to his wife so the faerie could look.

"Oh, Bethan," Healanie breathed. "She's perfect." She looked up at Rolf. "What are you naming her?"

"Well," Bethan began, "I was thinking..."

Rolf tried to signal to her with his eyes to stop, but this made Bethan simply look confused. This faerie had helped them in the end, but he was far too familiar with faerie gifts to want one here now, even if she did have the best interests of his people at heart. His family had received nearly all the blessings they could take.

"I don't think I told you this, Rolf," Healanie said, leaning toward the baby again and stroking her cheek, "but I gifted Bethan at birth as well."

This time, Rolf wasn't the only one who stared at her.

"You did?" Bethan asked.

Healanie grinned. "I did."

"What...what was it?" For the first time, Bethan seemed to feel the same anxiety that was currently overwhelming Rolf.

"An adventure." The faerie smiled again at the baby. "With a protector." Her grin widened. "That was you, Rolf."

Bethan turned to look at Rolf, her mouth open, though whether in horror or awe, Rolf couldn't tell.

"Please," Rolf said, finally finding his voice. "She doesn't need a gift. With the exception, of course, of your friendship—"

"Nonsense. You have both earned a gift for your child, many times over." The faerie pulled out her wand and held it in the air.

"Please," Rolf said again, trying to think quickly whether or not he could successfully snatch the baby up and run with her before the faerie began her work. "She's—"

"I will gift your daughter...something simple." The faerie tapped her cheek with her wand several times before nodding. "Yes. That's it. Something that will be a gift to not only herself but all those around her." She looked down at the baby and began swirling her wand over the child's head. Rolf watched in horror as the magic settled on the child and melted into her skin.

"What...what gift did you give her?" he asked, unable to tear his eyes away.

The faerie laughed. "No need to be afraid, Rolf. You learned your lesson. Her gift is something far better but no less powerful."

He looked up at the faerie once more. "What is that?"

The faerie smiled kindly. "Her gift is joy." And with that, in another puff of smoke, she was gone.

"I think," Bethan said softly, "we have found her name." She laughed a little. "It is a wonderful gift after all."

Rolf kissed his wife then his child, his heart ready to burst. He couldn't agree more.

The Enchanted Wreath

A Nevertold Fairy Tale Novella, Book #3

JULIEN BROUGHT his horse to a stop and looked around. "Where did she send us?" he muttered to his horse. "I don't know where we are, but it isn't the Regional Market."

He'd been following the road for two hours now, half an hour longer than it should have taken him to reach the largest market in the kingdom. He'd been to the market before, of course, but when Mother Dove had promised him that a little side road would be a shortcut, he hadn't stopped to question whether or not she knew what she was doing.

Mother Dove always knew what she was doing.

Which made him wonder all the more what she was up to.

"Perhaps she's punishing me for some new offense," he told his horse. "Now I just need to figure out what I've done this time." His horse only turned his head enough to give him an unimpressed glance.

"Well, there's water over there. We might as well get you a drink." Julien dismounted and led the horse to a bubbling little brook.

Well, if Mother Dove was going to punish him, at least she'd gotten him lost in one of the prettiest places Julien had ever seen. The world around him had exploded into every shade of green imaginable, from the wild grass to the leaves to the pine needs on the evergreens. Flower buds of blue, pink, and yellow were everywhere, and the brook sang happily as it tumbled against the rocks. Young stalks of some sort of new crop were beginning to grow in perfectly ordered fields in the distance, and the sky was an endless blue. As lovely as it all was, though, it still wasn't the Regional Market.

While his horse drank, Julien went back to the road.

"All right!" he called loudly. "Tell me what I've done so I can apologize for it. Then please put me back on the right path!"

There was no answer.

"Mother Dove!" he called out again. "I really do need to meet with Lord Hibbins."

If Mother Dove heard him, she didn't make a sound. With a huff, Julien walked back to his horse and was about to mount him again when a voice caught his attention. It was a woman's voice, and she was singing. He paused to listen, and after some seconds, realized that the woman's voice was accompanied by...were those birds?

Slowly, Julien led his horse through the trees and brush

toward the voice. If Mother Dove wasn't going to help him, he might as well get help from someone else.

The sound of an axe on wood echoed through the valley as well, and it seemed to be coming from the same direction as the voice, its loud crack accenting the beats of the song.

Finally, Julien made his way around a particularly large tree to find a young woman standing in a small clearing, splitting small logs on a large wooden stump.

The song she sang was lighthearted and quick, but even more amazing was that a number of birds--which he couldn't see--seemed to be harmonizing with her. The girl wore a common work dress, but on her head was the loveliest wreath of roses he'd ever seen. As intriguing as it was impractical for woodcutting.

The girl straightened and looked around. When she saw him, she dropped a quick curtsey then shouldered her axe, looking somewhat suspicious.

"Can I help you?" she asked, her brow slightly furrowed.

He could only guess that being a young woman all alone in the wood with a stranger would give her reason to be suspicious. He removed his hat and bowed low. "My apologies for interrupting." Hopefully, he hadn't frightened her.

Her sharp gaze traveled up and down his clothing. She had curtsied, so it was likely that she knew he was of higher rank simply due to the cut and quality of his clothes and his horse. But he doubted she knew what he really was, as her curtsey hadn't been particularly deep. He almost smiled to himself. All the better.

"How can I help you?" she asked again.

255

"I'm loathe to say it," he said, grinning sheepishly as he held his hat in his hands. "But I'm afraid I'm lost."

Her brow unfurrowed slightly. "Oh. Well, where are you looking to go?"

"The Regional Market. I was told this road was a shortcut."

"No," she said slowly, frowning again, "I'm afraid you're nowhere near the Regional Market. In fact...where did you come from?"

"The capital city," he said vaguely.

"If that's the case, you've been going in the opposite direction all morning. It's a good eight-hour walk from here." She glanced behind him. "Though, I'm not sure what it would take on a horse."

Julien stared at her then shook his head and laughed.

"What's so funny?" she asked.

He continued to chuckle. "It seems I was given the wrong directions on purpose." Julien wasn't in the habit of taking directions from animals. But Mother Dove wasn't just any animal. And she, more than any, would know whether or not the road she sent him down would be a shortcut. No faerie-blessed animal would make that mistake.

"If you're looking for the right road," the girl said, resting her axe on the stump, "you can cut through my father's field here." She pointed to the south. "Then you'll find a small dusty path that leads up to Shadeling. If you follow Shadeling's main road, you'll reach a fork in the road in about an hour. The road to the right will take you back to the capital city. The one to the left will take you to the market."

"I thank you." He bowed again and turned to his horse. Then he stopped. If Mother Dove had sent him this far, he might as well have a rest. And he had the sudden desire to rest near this pretty girl.

"Would you mind if I rest here for a few moments?" He gestured to his horse. "My horse would like to graze before we begin again."

She studied him for a long moment before nodding. "Very well." Then she bent and grabbed another small log.

He studied her unabashedly as she worked. She wasn't beautiful in the contrived way most noblewomen were. But there was a raw attractiveness to her, a natural pleasantness that made him wish to look more. Her eyes, a pale blue, were bright and sharp, and her long brown hair flowed unfettered down her shoulders and back as though she didn't care what it did. She was of average height and looked slightly underfed, but she was also strong, a strength he guessed that came with cutting wood.

"What's your name?" he asked.

"Gisele," she said before smashing the axe down on a piece of log. A long crack formed down the center. Then she straightened and wiped her forehead with her arm. "And who, might I ask, are you?"

Julien laughed without thinking. Her eyes widened slightly when he started laughing, but that only made it all the more humorous. She was bold, this little woodcutter. Most young women saw the quality of his clothes and either burst into simpering giggles or seductive charms. This girl, while polite, seemed to have either neither time nor interest in either of those reactions. She really seemed to have no idea who he was.

"Emile," he said. It wasn't a lie. Emile was his second name.

The girl--Gisele--nodded politely. "It is good to meet you, Emile." Then she went back to her cutting.

Julien watched her a moment longer before standing and taking the axe from her.

"Excuse me, sir!" she stared up at him indignantly. "What do you think you're doing?"

"I'm going to split logs for a bit, and you're going to sit and eat."

She stared at him as if he'd grown horns. "You're going to...what?"

"What I just said. I'll cut. You eat."

She flushed slightly. "I haven't anything to eat." Then she raised her chin. "And pardon the assumption, but what would a fine young gentleman such as yourself know of chopping wood?"

Julien raised one eyebrow, and took a larger piece of wood from the pile. Then he placed it on the stump upon which she'd been cutting and raised the axe above his head. Gisele hurried backward as he brought it crashing down, the two halves of the wood flying in opposite directions.

The look she gave him made him privately determine to thank his swords master when he got home. The man had forced him to chop wood to strengthen his shoulders when he was young. As a thirteen-year-old boy, he'd resented it with every fiber of his being. He had wanted to learn swords, and wood cutting was a skill he'd been sure would waste away forever. Clearly, his thirteen-year-old self had been mistaken.

"Well," Gisele said, clearing her throat slightly. "I...judged wrongly."

Julien smirked then nodded at his horse. "If you look in the saddlebags on the left side, you'll find more than enough food for both of us. Take it out and eat as much as you want while I do this."

The girl seemed hesitant to agree, but eventually, the invisible birds began to twitter anxiously, as if in a dream, she slowly turned and did as he said.

A few minutes later, a vast spread of food was laid out on a large rock nearby, and she was staring at it as though she wasn't sure what to do.

He grabbed another log. "If you don't mind me asking, why don't you have any food?" It was a rather intrusive question and probably impolite. But, Julien argued with himself, what good was having power if you couldn't use it to learn how your people fared? He'd been to the village she'd mentioned--Shadeline--only a few days before, and the people had seemed well-fed enough. Unless there was another crop blight he was unaware of. If so, he would need to alert his father.

"My...stepmother sent me none," she said hesitantly, gazing longingly at the food.

Julien paused long enough to grab and apple and take a

bite before putting it back down and taking another log. "Eat. Then tell me why your stepmother sent you no food." As the words came out of his mouth, he realized how commanding they sounded. Of course, that was how he spoke and was expected to speak at home. But out here, it just sounded overbearing.

Gisele frowned up at him slightly, seeming to think the same thing, when three little birds flew out of her wreath and began pecking at her hands.

"Fine! Fine!" she said, gently shooing at them with her hands. "I'll eat! But it's your fault if I get poisoned." Seeming satisfied, the little birds flew back up to her wreath and immediately nestled into it again.

Julien realized he was staring and forced himself to focus on the wood. He was getting more and more curious about this girl. But he'd better stick with one topic of conversation at a time.

"Is your family struggling?" he asked gently.

Gisele hesitated slightly before taking a small bite of bread. The way she briefly closed her eyes and sighed told him how hungry she really was. Then she opened her eyes and shrugged. "I offended her."

He stopped cutting. "So she gave you no food?" Cutting was hard work. Already, he was being reminded of how long it had been since his swords master had made him cut, and he liked to think himself in excellent health and strength. This girl was two heads shorter than he was and weighed far less. He couldn't imagine how hungry she must be after a full morning of such work.

Gisele kept her eyes on the bread. "My father is away." As if that explained it.

He put the axe down. "And will you tell your father when he returns?"

"I will, but I don't think he'll choose to hear."

Julien continued to study her, anger beginning to swirl in the pit of his stomach. He didn't know the girl well, of course. But if what she said was true, and he saw no reason to doubt her, Gisele was in a terrible situation.

Could he help her?

He could help her, of course, by ordering soldiers to haul the family away for mistreating her so. But then what would be left for her? The life of a lone, unwed woman was difficult and dangerous. He could give her a job in his home, of course, but...was that what she really wanted? To become a servant?

He decided he should get to know her first before he foisted his good intentions onto her without her permission. Her first inclination to his proffered help always seemed to be withdrawal. She was obviously quite self-reliant, and probably with good reason. Push too hard, and he could easily scare her away.

"I have another question," he said, trying to sound casual again. "Where did you get that wreath?"

She froze briefly, but before she could speak, the little birds within it began to tweet as though they were shouting. Gisele glanced up, then gave him a wry smile.

"Very well. I'll tell you. But only if you eat, too."

As his stomach was growling, he stuck the axe into the

stump, then joined her on the large flat rock. As they ate, she told him about her night in the storm and how she couldn't be sure, but she thought she'd dreamed about the voices of birds. Then, when she'd awakened, she was wearing this flower wreath, and now wherever she went, the birds went, too.

From the way she hesitated several times during the retelling, Julien got the feeling that she wasn't telling him everything. The way her family had treated her during the storm was even more reprehensible than not sending her food, and it made him wonder what other awful things they had done to her. But as soon as she began to describe the mother bird's words in her dream, Julien nearly laughed out loud. His strange morning suddenly made sense.

Mother Dove had wanted him to meet Gisele.

Find out whether Julien and Gisele find their happily-ever-after in the next book, The Enchanted Wreath: A Clean Fantasy Fairy Tale Retelling of The Enchanted Wreath.

Dear Reader,
Thank you for reading The Prince's Dangerous Wish.
If you'd like more (free) happily-ever-afters, visit
BrittanyFichterFiction.com, where my subscribers get free,

exclusive stories, sneak peeks at books before they're published, coupon codes, and much more.

Also, if you liked the book, it would be a huge help to me if you could leave an honest review on your favorite ebook retailer or Goodreads so others can find this story, too!

ABOUT THE AUTHOR

Brittany lives with her Prince Charming, their little fairy, and their little prince in a ~~sparkling~~ (decently clean) castle in whatever kingdom the Air Force has most recently placed them. When she's not writing, Brittany can be found chasing her kids around with a DSLR and belting it in the church choir.

Subscribe: BrittanyFichterFiction.com
Email: BrittanyFichterFiction@gmail.com
Facebook: Facebook.com/BFichterFiction
Instagram: @BrittanyFichterFiction

THE PRINCE'S DANGEROUS WISH: A CLEAN FANTASY FAIRY TALE RETELLING OF THE PINK

Copyright © 2023 Brittany Fichter

Brittany Fichter. -- 1st ed.

Cover Design by Moor Books Design

Edited by Theresa Emms

Made in the USA
Middletown, DE
01 October 2023